AF579616

The Guardian: Special Edition

Delta's Story

Kathryn Braddock

Copyright © 2022 Kathryn Braddock

All rights reserved.

ISBN: 979-8368160801

DEDICATION

To Ms Katy,

Just as Delta is a mentor to Willow,
you are a mentor to me.

PROLOGUE

Oriole went to sleep in his chamber, but when he awoke he stood in a forest.

The Crystal Forest.

The red-furred wolf knew what that meant. The Stone must have a prophecy!

The sparkling pond glittered before him. Crouching low on his paws, Oriole peered down into it.

His eyes widened at what he saw. A picture could be seen through the water, of a tiny gray she-pup with dazzling blue eyes. This must be the one.

The next leader of the Guardians.

"When is she coming?" He whispered.

A new picture appeared, of a she-wolf that looked just like the pup.

"Mistflower," Oriole murmured. "She and Birch are about to have pups. This future leader is coming soon!"

He turned to see a pulsing bright light coming closer and closer. "Thank you for this prophecy. I've been waiting for her a long time" *I will wait until she is older to tell any of her destiny, besides the Power-Holders.*

1

“Cynthia! Poppy! Wait for me!” I called as my paws slipped on the cold stone. My two sisters vanished up the tunnel that led to the Crystal Cavern.

This was our first day to leave the little chamber we had been born in. We were going to meet the rest of the Guardians!

“Come on, Mother!” I squeaked at the silver-furred she-wolf that stood nearby. “Father’s waiting for us!”

“Yes, he is,” Mistflower, my mother, said with a chuckle. She followed behind as we sisters rushed up the tunnel.

I banged into Cynthia as they both stood just out of sight of the Crystal Cavern. Their eyes were as wide as mine as we heard the commotion outside the tunnel we stood in.

"What are you waiting for?" Mistflower asked gently, nudging Poppy forward.

The copper-colored wolf scooted back. "Nothing. It's just *so* noisy in there!"

I felt scared as well, but Father was out there! I wanted to show him that at least *one* of his pups was brave!

I marched past my sisters, and the light blinded me for a moment.

The Crystal Cavern was huge! Crystals were set along the roof and walls, giving off an unearthly blue glow. A waterfall cascaded down, ending in a small pond. Arches of stone crossed the water, leading to a platform that floated atop the gentle water. And on top of that platform, rising to the Cavern's roof…

The Guardian Stone was beautiful! I had heard Mistflower speak of how it was our duty to protect it, and that it was the source of all light. I'd wondered how a simple stone could be so impressive.

And here it was, so impressive.

My attention shifted to the crowd of wolves that gathered in the Crystal Cavern. Their eager eyes shone as they saw me, and their tails wagged.

I felt overwhelmed at first, but then I saw Birch, my father, his eyes filled with pride. Then I raised my head high, standing as tall as I could with my short legs. Cynthia and Poppy crept up on either side of me, awe plain in their eyes.

"It's beautiful," Poppy whispered.

Mistflower let out a rumble of laughter. "Welcome to the Guardians."

"Cynthia, Poppy." A majestic dark red wolf with piercing green eyes stepped towards us.

My own blue eyes widened. This was obviously Oriole, leader of the Guardians. Around him, nine other wolves stepped forward. The Power-Holders!

Oriole dipped his head, eyes landing on me. "Delta." His wise eyes glowed. "Welcome to the Guardians."

An elder wolf with dark gray fur craned her head to get a look at us. "I bet they'll be talented at fighting," she called out in a raspy voice, "just like their parents. They may even have what it takes to be a Power-Holder in training!"

The wolves around her yipped in excited agreement, stomping their paws.

My insides churned. Cynthia was great at fighting, even at five moons old. She would become a fierce warrior. Poppy was always really kind, and seemed to have an acute sense of the world around her. She could be a Power-Holder. But me? *I'm good at those things, but not* as *good.*

Oriole was now walking back into the crowd of wolves. My sisters began whispering in excitement about what to explore first, but I was too worried. Would I be special?

I wanted to be, truly.

I stared at the stone wall as my sisters and I settled into our bracken beds. We still weren't old enough to sleep in the Sleeping Chamber, where adult wolves slept, as well as pups six moon old and above. "I wonder if any of us really *does* have a special future, like that elder wolf— I think her name was Fern— said."

"I know!" Poppy squealed from the darkness. Then she stiffened, casting a glance at the shadowy form of Mistflower, who slept nearby.

"I'm going to be leader of the fighting force one day," Cynthia spoke up. She shook out her cream-colored coat. "Either that or leader of *everything.*"

I snorted. "There's no such thing as a leader of the fighting force."

"So?" She puffed out her chest. "I'll be the first."

There was silence for a moment, then Poppy spoke up. "While you were sitting around, Delta, and while Cynthia was exploring, I met someone." Her voice was a little nervous.

I traded a skeptical glace with Cynthia, then returned my gaze to Poppy. *"Who?"*

My copper-furred sister mumbled her next words. "A young wolf, only ten moons older than us. His name was—"

"HIS?!" Cynthia and I both shouted. Mistflower stirred, but surprisingly did not wake. I stared at my sister earnestly. "You should have told us sooner, Poppy. We are your older sisters, after all."

"By only *three* minutes!" She hissed.

Cynthia giggled. "What was *his* name?"

"Peak." Poppy's eyes were shining. "His name was Peak. He has really smooth, dark gray fur, and pale green eyes. He showed me around."

I rolled my eyes, while Cynthia muttered, "yuck."

"Why don't you introduce us to this *Peak* tomorrow?" I said. "I want to check him out."

"Seriously," Poppy groaned, "he's just a new wolf I've met! He's really nice! You'll see."

"We will," Cynthia responded as the three of us settled down.

The next day found us standing in the Crystal Cavern.

"There he is!" Poppy's voice was extremely nervous. Her paws shifted as Cynthia and I looked around eagerly. "Maybe we could meet him later?" She suggested timidly.

"No. Now." I pushed past her, striding purposefully through the throng of wolves, towards a gray pup that was playing with a small stone.

"Gotcha!" He slapped his paws over the pebble. "Another deer caught by Peak!"

"Ahem." I cleared my throat loudly, Cynthia right behind me. Poppy padded cautiously a little ways behind.

The pup looked up. His green eyes met mine, and I felt a flash of surprise. They were not the shade I'd been expecting. This color was kind of murky.

But despite the dull hue of his eyes, they still sparkled with laughter. I began to see how he must have stolen my sister's sweet, unsuspecting heart at first sight.

I was not easily put at ease by his innocent act, though.

"Peak." I sat down on my haunches, barely a tail length away from him.

Peak tilted his head. "Hi!" He said cheerfully. "I see you already know my name!" Then his eyes grew worried. "You're one of the new pups! It's a little drafty in here today. Maybe you should be in your den."

I struggled not to roll my eyes. "I might be a pup, buddy, but so are you. Stop acting like I'm made of crystal."

Poppy let out a gasp of horror, and even Cynthia seemed a little taken aback by my straightforward manner.

But not Peak. The sparkle in his eyes only grew brighter. "Sorry, Delta— that's your name, right?" He swept his tail from side to side. "It's nice to meet you." Then his eyes landed on Poppy. "Hi! It's good to see you again!"

"Thanks," Poppy stammered, her pelt ruffling under his gaze. I forced back a snicker. "I brought my sisters, Cynthia and Delta, to meet you!"

Peak nodded, then turned enthusiastically to greet Cynthia. I actually did snicker as my sister marched up to face him, snout to snout.

"You seem like the prankster type," she said in a threatening voice, "you should know that I do not like to be pranked." She stomped one of her tiny paws to show how serious she was.

Peak was not deterred. "Don't worry," he said breezily, "I won't prank you three." Then his eyes lit up even more. "Do you want to go look at the Guardian Stone? I haven't tried to cross the arches yet, but I'm sure we're allowed to!"

I was sure Poppy was about to faint from excitement. "Fine," I spoke before either of my sisters could, "but if we get in trouble it's on you."

"Then come on!" He scampered over to where the stone floor dropped away, giving way to a deep pool of water always supplied by the waterfall. No wolf knew where any of this structure had come from, but yesterday Fern had told me that this place was built by light itself. After that, the Guardian Stone was formed as a home for the light, and the first Guardian wolf began living here in High Mountain.

"Delta, come on!" Cynthia called. She, Poppy, and Peak were already crawling across the stone arches that ran over the water to the stone platform.

"Coming." I placed one paw onto the bridge. It seemed stable. I placed another paw on, until I found myself in the center of the arch. That's when I looked down.

Dark water pulsated with energy beneath me. I froze, imagining its icy chill creeping past my thick gray fur and freezing my bones. I suddenly couldn't move.

"Delta?" Peak called to me. They were already standing on the arch, at the base of the Stone. "Are you okay?"

I gritted my teeth, not wanting to show any weakness. Trembling slightly, I began walking forward. To my relief, the bridge did not crumble. "Phew!" I panted, flattening my small body against the stone platform.

"Don't worry, Delta!" Peak blinked at me reassuringly. "Heavier wolves than you have crossed that bridge!" His voice grew softer. "*Way* heavier."

I stiffened as he pointed with his muzzle at a plump elder wolf that was on the other side of the water. "Shh!" I hissed, surprised he would talk about an elder wolf like that. "Are you *trying* to get us in trouble?"

Peak shook out his gray fur, clearly not panicked. "Who would get us in trouble?" he said boldly.

"Uh, let me think!" Cynthia stuck her muzzle in his face. "Maybe *Oriole!*"

"Peak can say whatever he wants!" Poppy cut in, then ducked her head.

While all that continued, my eyes caught on something. The Guardian Stone stood erect, just a few feet away. I stepped up to it, seeing my reflection in the smooth blue crystal. The stone seemed to glow brighter than all the crystals in the Crystal Cavern combined.

"It's beautiful," I felt Poppy's breath near my ear as she too stared at the Stone. Cynthia and Peak were arguing, but their voices slowly faded as all my senses delved into the Guardian Stone.

I could hear a slight rushing sound, like a waterfall. I could see bright, pulsating colors on every side. I could smell a scent that seemed to me like a fresh breeze. I could taste a cold, metallic presence on my tongue. I could feel myself falling through air that wasn't air.

I found myself standing in a bright, sunny forest. The dirt was firm beneath my paws, and the trees swayed gently in the wind. I found I could not move, but I could look around.

Suddenly time seemed to fast forward. I was in the same forest, but this time it was dark and decayed.

Dark shapes rushed past me, howling in terror and pain. Red shone out on their dark pelts.

"Are you okay?" I shouted, as three wolves stopped near me, their eyes wide with fear. "Do you need help? What's happening?!" But they just stared right through me.

"We have to do something!" One of them, a young black she-wolf, stamped her paws.

"We can't!" The second wolf, a young russet male, cried. "The darkness is too strong!"

"Shade!" The she-wolf whirled to face the third wolf, an older brown male. "Surely you have ideas!"

"I do." Shade lifted his graying muzzle. "We must dive into the core of the darkness. The light will protect us."

"But what will we do when we reach it?" The young male wolf shouted over the screaming wind.

"We will know when the time comes!" Shade rumbled. All three of them turned as an eerie scream filled the air. "The darkness has come!"

I whirled around to see a giant, pulsating wave of shadow rising over the forest. It blotted out the moon, and whatever it touched shriveled. Fear coursed through my veins. What was that?!

"Go! And may the light guide our paws!" Shade charged forward. The two young wolves took off after him. A soft glow began to outline their bodies, then they vanished into the darkness.

I gasped in horror as I was pulled towards it. "No!" I cried. "Mistflower!" But I was swallowed by the shadowy form, unharmed.

I stood on the outskirts of the center of the darkness, a sickening void that sucked all light. The three wolves stood close by, struggling to keep the light they had created.

"We must destroy it!" The black she-wolf howled. She lifted her muzzle bravely. "For all the world!" Then she plunged into the heart of the darkness.

"Willow!" The russet male screeched, pain etched all over his face as the she-wolf's agonized screams filled the air.

"Quickly, Copper!" Shade shouted. "We must follow Willow! The light of three Guardians can be used to push the darkness back to wherever it came from!"

Copper nodded. "Then we will sacrifice ourselves to save the world!" They plunged in after Willow.

My pelt spiked as the three wolves' shrieks split through my body. The wall of darkness around me gave one jarring shudder, then imploded on Shade, Copper, and Willow.

Then I stood once more in the sunny forest. But this time something was different. Bodies and blood lay scattered, and where the heart of the darkness had been, three sets of wolf paw prints were engraved into a stone.

2

My vision grew black for a second, then I found myself standing once more in front of the Guardian Stone. No time seemed to have passed— Cynthia and Peak were still arguing, and Poppy still gazed at the Stone.

My breath came in frantic gasps. I realized that my fur was bushed up, and I was digging my claws into the stone platform.

"Delta?" My copper-colored sister was looking at me, worry in her brown eyes. "Are you okay?" Peak and Cynthia were staring at me.

I relaxed, not meeting their eyes. "Yeah," I lied, "I just felt a chilly draft of air. I'm going to go see if Mistflower can get me something to eat." Then I rushed over the stone arch, not even noticing the water this time. All I felt was terror at what I had just witnessed.

Had the Stone given *me* a vision?

"Are you feeling alright, Delta? You've seemed distant ever since yesterday." Mistflower's blue eyes sparkled with worry for me, as she entered our small den with a chunk of meat. She set it down at my paws.

"I'm feeling fine," I replied. That was mostly true— I felt great physically. Unfortunately, the mental part of my being was not doing so well.

My mother sighed. "Then try to be more cheerful. Young wolves are the future of the Guardians."

I remembered the strange vision from yesterday. "What if one day there is no future?"

Mistflower gave me a sharp look. "Delta, that's the most morbid thing I've ever heard, especially coming from a pup! Of course there's a future. The Guardians have thrived in the past, present, and future."

I chewed on the mountain goat meat that lay at my paws, nodding as my mother continued. But my mind was elsewhere. I was afraid of the future, but more so of the past, for surely the vision was from long ago? My pelt pricked with unease. What if the terrible darkness returned? Who would stop it? I had never fully understood what it meant to be a Guardian. Now I had an idea.

"Ow!" I shrieked as Cynthia's claws snagged my fur. "Cynthia, be careful! We're not trying to murder each other!"

My sister stepped off me, looking sheepish. "Sorry, Delta. I just got carried away."

"But you're a great fighter!" Peak chirped from outside the fighting boundaries.

"Yeah!" Poppy chimed in from where she sat at his side.

"Easy for you guys to say," I grumbled, shaking out my long gray fur, "you're not the ones she's beating up."

"Look!" Cynthia broke up the impending debate. "There's Oriole!"

We all turned to see the old Guardian leader padding from the tunnel that led to his chamber.

"He looks tired," I commented.

"Well, yeah!" Peak replied, a little too loudly. "He's got lots of stuff to take care of."

Cynthia rose onto her back legs and waved her forepaws in the air. "Like fighting dangerous things?"

"Like bad wolves!" Poppy exclaimed, her eyes huge. "Fern says that she fought a mean wanderer once, when she was young and hadn't yet entered the Guardians."

"When I grow up, I'm going to wipe all darkness off the face of the earth!" Peak said, his eyes narrow. "I'll be a hero!"

I began laughing, but it died in my throat as I realized Oriole was watching *me.*

What was that look in our leader's eyes? It gave me chills, like he knew something we didn't.

"Pups!" I whirled to see that Birch was padding towards us. "Oriole and the Power-Holders have decided that you three are to be tested now."

"Tested?" Poppy sounded scared. "By what?"

Birch's eyes held pride. "By the Guardian Stone, of course."

3

"What?!" I stared at my father. *"The Guardian Stone?"*

Peak let out a squeak of excitement. "The Stone can be used to determine whether a pup might have a future as a Power-Holder!" His tail drooped. "I flunked."

"Yay!" Cynthia squealed, bouncing around Birch. "Let's go!"

He chuckled. "Go over the arches and to the Stone."

My insides churned. "You're not going with us?"

"I'll be on the other side of the pond," he told me. "Only the Power-Holders, including Oriole, are allowed to be next to the Stone while you're tested."

"Go on!" Peak urged us. A crowd was already forming in the Crystal Cavern. "It'll feel weird, but not too bad."

I shivered as Cynthia, Poppy, and I made our way through the crowd, over the arches, and up to the Guardian Stone. Nine wolves already waited on the platform. I glanced around. Where was the Guardian leader?

Then he padded out from behind the Stone, his fur shining, despite his obvious age.

"Today is a special day!" he called. "We will test three pups. Any of them could have what it takes to be a Power-Holder, or even…" His tone grew serious as he turned to us. "A future leader. Of course, if one of them is destined for *that,* we will find out much later."

Sunshine, one of the Power-Holders, stepped forward. "Cynthia, step up to the Stone."

My cream-furred sister eagerly stepped up to the Guardian Stone.

"Guardian Stone, source of light," the Power-Holders began chanting, "show if this wolf's destined to receive your might."

Cynthia rose up onto the tips of her paws in excitement.

Nothing happened.

"Young Cynthia," Oriole flicked his tail kindly, "it seems that your future does not hold this position. You will find your calling elsewhere. You will be a fierce warrior."

Cynthia's tail drooped in disappointment, but she nodded, stepping back to where Poppy and I waited.

Sunshine spoke once more. "Delta, step forward to the Stone."

At first my paws were paralyzed with fear. *What's wrong with me?* Every wolf waited expectantly, but I was frozen.

Then I saw Peak on the other side of the water. His eyes held disappointment for Cynthia, but there was something else… certainty. He knew that I could do it. He believed in me.

With a deep breath, I stepped up to the Guardian Stone. Fear fluttered in my belly. What if I had another scary vision? What if Oriole decided that I wasn't worth testing? What if—

"Guardian Stone, source of light, show if this wolf's destined to receive your might." The chant had already started!

I thought I might retch as the half-seconds dragged on. Then my fur shimmered slightly. The wolves filling the Crystal Cavern burst into cheers.

"She's to be a Power-Holder in training!" Oriole howled over the din. "She may not receive a position, but at least she's one of our options!"

"Delta! Delta! Delta!" Hundreds of voices cried. My eyes widened with surprise. I had made it through the test. I *was* special!

Then I once more stood with my sisters, and it was Poppy's turn. Her copper-colored fur was bushed out, and her brown eyes betrayed her fear.

"Guardian Stone, source of light, show if this wolf's destined to receive your might."

Poppy's fur began to glow, just as mine had. But then she was lifted into the air, and her eyes glowed.

Every wolf in the Crystal Cavern gasped in surprise. I saw that Oriole's eyes were huge. What was wrong with my sister?

I began to step forward in panic, but then Poppy fell back to the ground, looking like a normal pup once more.

The Guardians erupted into whispering. Only Oriole and the other nine Power-Holders seemed to understand what had just happened. They stared at Poppy in awe.

"What?" My pup sister sat up, looking confused. "What happened? Did I make it?"

Oriole strode towards her, clearing his throat. "Poppy has been born with magic from the Stone."

Howls of surprise echoed through the Cavern. "But that's not possible!" Fern croaked. "Right?"

Oriole shook his head. "I didn't think so. But we have seen it— Poppy has strong Lostina. She will undoubtedly be a Power-Holder someday."

"Why not leader?" a wolf called. I heard Poppy squeak in terror.

Oriole seemed to be uncomfortable about something. "The Guardian Stone hasn't sent me any signs about her," he said at last. "For now, Poppy will be trained by our Power-Holders, separate from the other young wolves. She must learn to harness her powers."

I could imagine the terror my sister must feel— she would have to be trained alone. She had never really liked being set apart.

I felt a tinge of envy. Poppy was *super* special. I pushed it away. So what? I was going to be trained as well! I felt disappointment for Cynthia, but it was forgotten as the Guardian leader met my eyes. "Delta, *your* training starts tomorrow. If you work hard, you might someday be a Power-Holder alongside your sister."

I nodded determinedly. I was going to work harder than any other wolf to become the best Power-Holder I could be.

4

"Delta! Wake up!" Tiny paws thumped into my side.

I rolled over with a groan. "Stop it."

"But you can't sleep in!" Poppy's voice was urgent. "You'll be late for training!"

My eyes shot open, and I leaped out of my leafy bed. "Oh yeah! I can't wait!"

"Yeah," Poppy fidgeted nervously, "can't wait."

I placed a paw on her shoulder. "You'll do fine! Which Power-Holder is teaching you today?"

"Breeze," she replied. "She seems really nice, so I'm hoping we don't try something too bad."

"Where's Cynthia?" I looked around our chamber. Mistflower was there, but my other sister was nowhere to be seen.

Poppy wagged her tail. "Some of the strongest Guardians asked if she wanted to learn how to fight! She left not long ago."

"Yay!" I felt excitement for her. She would like learning to fight more than magic, most likely. Then I stared at Poppy. "So, can you use your magic?"

She shook her head. "No. I can feel it inside of me, but I can't use it. Well, I'd better go. Bye, Delta!"

"Good luck, Poppy!" I shouted after her as she raced up the tunnel, passing Birch on the way.

"My little pups," my father said, pride in his voice.

"They are going to be the strongest Guardians to ever walk the earth," Mistflower replied, rising from her bed.

I ducked my head. "Not the *strongest.*" I thought about the three wolves in my vision, which seemed like it had happened so long ago, though it was only days ago. If any wolves were the strongest, it was *them.* I couldn't even imagine being brave enough to sacrifice myself to the darkness.

"You should hurry." Mistflower nudged me towards the tunnel. "Follow the other young wolves. They will lead you to the Training Cave."

"You'll do wonderful," Birch added. "You just need to believe in yourself, Delta, like the rest of us. *We* believe in you."

"Thanks." I hurried into the Crystal Cavern, joining the other young Power-Holders in training as they padded towards a tunnel I had never been down before.

I gulped. I was the youngest wolf here. All the other pups were so much older than me!

We entered a large cave, pillars of stone holding up the roof. A slab of stone rose a little higher than the ground. I guessed that was where the Power-Holder that was teaching us would sit.

All the wolves began to sit around the slab. I hung back, a little nervous. Would there even be any room for me?

"Here!" A she-pup with blonde fur and dark eyes was calling to me. She seemed to be ten moons old. "You can sit next to me!"

I blinked at her gratefully, then stepped cautiously through the group of wolves, heading for her. I accidently bumped into a black wolf on the way. She turned to me with a growl. "Watch it, pup."

"Be nice, Sky!" The blonde-furred pup snapped loudly. "You're still a pup too, you know!"

"I'm twenty-three moons old!" Sky snarled. "In one moon I'll be an adult!"

The nice she-pup rolled her eyes, then glanced at me. "Ignore her. She likes to pick on younger wolves."

"Thanks for standing up for me," I said earnestly, sitting next to her. "I really want to try and fit in."

"You already do!" she said cheerfully. "I'm Lemon!"

My nerves calmed a bit. "I'm Delta."

At that moment, one of the Power-Holders entered the Training Cave, stepping up to the platform.

"I am Stone." he announced. His name fit— he had gray fur. "Today, since we have a new student, we will review." He nodded at me. "Welcome, Delta. I trust you will listen and study hard, and will make us proud."

I dipped my head enthusiastically. "Yes, Stone!"

Sky snickered at my eagerness. Lemon shot her a glare, and I felt a flash of gratitude towards the older pup.

Stone didn't seem to notice Sky's rudeness. "You are Guardians. It is your duty to protect the Guardian Stone. In other words, you must watch over the light, making sure it is never snuffed out. Today we are going to review Lostina. Who can tell me what it is?"

"It's what gives wolves their thoughts!" Lemon called out. "It is what gives us life other than our own. Without it, we would not be one with nature. We would be thoughtless."

"Excellent answer, Lemon," Stone swished his tail. "You are correct. Lostina dwells within every wolf. The spirit of a wolf is incomplete without it. But, it is possible for wolves to be given more, so that it can be turned into power. Usually a wolf must earn it." His eyes rested on me. "But, as seen in the case of Delta's sister, it is possible for a wolf to be born with strong Lostina."

"The only explanation for that is that the Guardian Stone gave her the power," a gray male pup with white flecks in his fur piped up, "that the light chose to give it to her."

"Exactly, Reed," Stone paced along the edge of the platform, "but the question is this— *why?* Why was

Poppy, a she-pup of five moons, born with strong Lostina? Is there something in the future that requires her to have it? Only time will tell."

I realized I had been holding my breath. I let it out with a *whoosh*. Was Poppy destined for greatness? Were Cynthia and I special too? I had a vision!

I felt a rush of guilt. I should have probably told someone about what I had seen, but what if it sounded like I was trying to get attention?

Lemon nudged me, and I realized that Stone was once more talking. "As possible future Power-Holders, you all must be ready to serve the Guardians." I winced, wondering how much of his lesson I had just missed. He nodded down at us. "That is enough for today. Tomorrow you will learn more about Lostina, and even a chant. It will be taught by Sunshine." He looked out over the crowd of pups and young wolves. His eyes met mine, last of all. "You are all dismissed."

"Goodbye, Delta!" Lemon told me, wagging her bushy tail. "It was great to meet you!"

"Thanks!" I replied cheerfully. "See you tomorrow!"

Sky pushed past us, heading for the exit. I glared after her. Why did she have to be so mean?

I left the Training Cave, meeting up with Poppy, Cynthia, and Peak in the Crystal Cavern.

"Hi, Delta!" Cynthia squealed as I padded up. "I had so much fun learning different battle moves! Peak and a few other pups came, too! It was awesome!"

"Yeah!" Peak added. His eyes sparkled just as bright as ever. "It *was* fun, though Cynthia beat the rest of us in all our fake battles!"

"I had fun, too," I said, leaving out any mention of Sky. "I met a really nice pup called Lemon. Stone taught us about Lostina."

We all then turned to Poppy. "How did it go?" Cynthia asked eagerly.

My sister's ears flattened. "I had to try and use my magic to heal a small cut Breeze had. I tried and I tried but I couldn't do it."

I lowered my tail in sympathy. "Don't worry, Poppy. It was your first day. You'll get it eventually."

"Yeah," she sighed, "I really hope so." I thought about telling her what Stone had said about her future, but decided not to. Poppy didn't need any more stress.

5

A few days later, I was in the Training Cave once more.

"Vestina is a dark form of Lostina, used only by wolves with hearts as black as the darkest night," I answered the question Root, a Power-Holder, had hurled at us.

He shook out his russet fur, pleased. "Excellent, Delta. You are only five moons old, and yet you've become one of the smartest students here."

I sat taller, pride filling my body with warmth. Lemon nudged my shoulder happily. I could see Sky cast me an infuriated look. I loved being the best at everything!

"You think you're so smart!" Sky huffed as all the young wolves began leaving the Training Cave.

Lemon stepped in front of me. "Because she *is* smart, Sky! Smarter than you."

I cringed as the black she-wolf's gaze grew stormy. "I'm not smarter than any wolf," I said quietly.

Sky tossed her head. "Make sure it stays that way, Delta." She stalked away.

I sighed, turning to Lemon. "I really don't want to be her enemy."

The blonde she-pup shrugged. "Sky's always loved *pretending* to be the best. Well, I'll see you tomorrow, Delta."

"Okay." I left the Training Cave, meeting up with Poppy as she emerged from a tunnel shrouded in shadow.

"It's kind of creepy down there," she commented, "creepy, but cool."

My ears perked. "Really? May I see?"

She stared down at her paws. "I don't know if you're allowed."

"Let's go find Cynthia," I said after a moment's pause. I began padding towards the Crystal Cavern. I felt a nudge of worry for Poppy. She looked exhausted and disappointed. Was she *still* not able to use her Lostina? She hadn't talked about her training for a while, even when Cynthia and I tried to ask questions.

I just wished my sister wasn't so unhappy. She had an awesome power!

We padded the rest of the way in silence.

"Delta, Poppy," Cynthia greeted us as we emerged from the tunnel, "today I learned lots of cool moves. I really like fighting!"

"I'm glad," I replied, then glanced around. "Where's Peak?" The pup always seemed to cheer Poppy's spirits. Besides, it was funny to see my sister's awkwardness around him!

"Right here!" The gray pup raced up, almost colliding with Cynthia. "Sorry I'm late! Training made me hungry."

Just as I had thought, Poppy's tail wagged. "Hi, Peak! What do you want to do today?"

"Well…" Peak glanced around the Cavern, then lowered his voice. "I had a chance to leave the Guardian Caverns yesterday. I stood on the very top of High Mountain. It was awesome!" He paused for dramatic effect, then continued. "Do you three want to come?"

My eyes widened. "What!" Cynthia burst out, then whispered, "are you sure it's safe?"

"Of course," Peak said breezily, "My mother took me up there."

"She's coming?" I asked.

His head dropped guiltily. "Well, no. She doesn't know I plan to go out there again." His eyes lit up once more. "But it will be worth it, I promise."

"I'm in." My heart raced at the thought of being so high above the world.

"Delta, are you crazy?" Cynthia whirled to face me. "You are a Power-Holder in training! So is Poppy! You're expected not to get into trouble!"

"We won't," I assured her, "right, Poppy?"

The copper-furred pup looked nervous. "I guess so."

"Don't worry," Peak nudged her, "I'll protect you." Poppy seemed convinced, standing a little straighter.

Now our adventure depended on whether Cynthia would tell Mistflower or not.

The creamy-furred pup shifted her paws. "What about Oriole? He seems to know everything that goes on."

"This won't take long," I promised, "he won't notice."

I held my breath.

At last Cynthia let out a giant sigh. "Very well. But *I* can protect myself, and don't you ever forget that, Peak."

He nodded. "Let's go!"

It was pretty easy to slip into the largest tunnel unnoticed. I gazed down it nervously, feeling a chilly gust of wind. It was *so* dark!

Then Peak marched forward, Cynthia and Poppy at his heels. I plunged into the shadows.

I could hear the pups' voices up ahead, but they were faint. I was surrounded on all sides by darkness, just like in my vision. I was almost certain the shadows were shaped like wolves, following me with every step.

Panic took over, and I raced for the small light that could be seen up ahead, almost colliding with the others as I burst into the freshest air in the world.

I stood on a large snowy platform, surrounded by… clouds. The sun was just setting, sending rays of color in all direction.

My breath was gone as I gazed at the sight. Through the haze, I could make out a green smudge far below. That must be the swamp. I'd heard that one lay close to High Mountain.

"Beautiful, isn't it?" Peak's breath stirred the air beside my ear.

I turned to see him and my two sisters. Cynthia's eyes were popping with wonder, and Poppy looked like she was about to faint from excitement.

"Come on!" Peak began wading through the thin layer of snow that covered the mountain. "I want to go to the very edge. Mother wouldn't let me yesterday."

"But isn't that dangerous?" Poppy peered after him anxiously, but he gave no reply.

I rolled my eyes. "You know how stubborn male wolves are. Anyway, the view probably *is* far better at the edge." I trotted after my friend.

Peak sat at the edge of the mountain. My head spun a little as I saw how far the drop was. A fall would kill strongest of wolves, let alone a small pup!

But… it was an amazing view.

My eyes caught a flash of color, and I glanced down to see a large blue flower poking out of the snow, just a few feet down a steep slope. "Mistflower would love that!"

"Are you sure you can reach it, Delta?" Peak's eyes flashed with worry. "It's pretty far down."

"Yeah!" I said boldly. "A future Power-Holder needs to be brave! I've got this!" Carefully placing one paw in front of the other, I slowly inched downward, using my needle-like claws to grip the stone that lay buried beneath the snow.

"Delta!" Cynthia cried out angrily. "What are you *doing?"*

I didn't look back. I was so close to that flower. I imagined Mistflower's delight when I gave it to her, and how proud she would be of my bravery. My nose was full of the flower's sweet scent.

My ears began to buzz as the wind whipped at my small form. Was that Cynthia's voice again? *Why won't she just let me get this flower real quick?*

"DELTA!" Peak screeched.

Ignoring him, I stretched out my neck and gripped the flower between my teeth. It wouldn't come loose, so I gave it a little yank.

That's when I realized the stone beneath my paws was unsteady. I pitched forward.

"Nooo!" I screamed, lunging for a root that stuck up nearby. The stone I had been standing on slid down the mountain, vanishing into the haze.

The flower tickled the inside of my mouth, but I refused to let go of the root. I could see Peak, Cynthia, and Poppy up above me. They seemed to be howling something, but the wind was roaring. Then Poppy whirled around and vanished from view – to get help I hoped.

My jaw muscles were growing weary, burning with the effort. I couldn't hold on much longer. *If only I had strong Lostina!*

My eyes locked with Peak's. His face was twisted with guilt and terror. That was understandable. He *was* the reason I was now clinging to a root on the side of a mountain!

Then Poppy reappeared, but no one was with her. Hopelessness dashed against my consciousness. I was going to die!

Then a massive shadow covered me. I felt something hard grab me around my middle, and I was yanked away from the root and into the air.

I looked up to see a large hawk. Screeching in terror, I struggled desperately to break free of its cruel talons.

Then I was dropped safely to the ground beside Peak, Cynthia, and Poppy.

I whirled to face the bird but instead saw Oriole. "Leader! Did you see that? A hawk just saved my life!"

The Guardian leader's voice was icy. "That was me, Delta. My Lostina allows me to shape-shift."

I was about to say how neat that was, but then I noticed that he was glaring at me. Birch and Mistflower were there as well. Neither of my parents looked happy.

I realized that the flower was no longer in my mouth. I must have swallowed it. *Gross!*

"How *could* you?" Mistflower jabbed her muzzle at me. "Delta, you could have *died!*"

"That was *very* irresponsible!" Birch added.

My ears flattened. "I know. I…"

Peak rushed forward to stand in front of me, followed by my sisters. "It was my fault!" he blurted. "I wanted to come out here again! I convinced them to come!" Cynthia and Poppy added their own thoughts as well.

My tail drooped between my legs. "It was all of our faults. I'm sorry."

They voiced apologies as well, and Oriole's muzzle relaxed. "You are all forgiven, but this mistake will cost you four. The rest of this day will be spent cleaning anything that needs to be done."

"Yes, Oriole," I bowed my head, though I dreaded the rest of the day.

A future Power-Holder was supposed to be wise, wasn't she?

Then why have I just done something so stupid?

6

I sighed as I settled into my bed that night. Birch and Mistflower had been really angry, so we weren't allowed to eat dinner with the other pups.

I felt a flash of irritation. All this led to Peak. He was the reason we were in trouble. A tiny voice in my head told me it wasn't fair to blame him, but I pushed it away.

Cynthia was furious, which was no surprise – she'd been looking forward to showing off some battle moves to the other young wolves tonight.

Poppy was a little upset as well, though she tried not to show it.

I stretched my forelegs as I sank into sleep. It had been a long day. I was ready for rest…

"Delta!" A black she-wolf was howling. "You must do something!"

I raced towards her writhing form, but a tree fell into my path. The forest was burning. Soon nothing would be left.

"No!" I screeched as the wolf crumbled into ash. "I don't know what to do!"

Then it hit me. I had to find the source of the darkness!

Whirling, I ran towards a black cloud that was stretching over the earth.

Droplets of rain hit my pelt, soon becoming a torrent. I was still running, but my paws were going nowhere.

The water washed through my thick gray fur, until it felt that I was drowning.

My eyes flew open and I sat bolt upright in my bracken bed, gasping.

My fur was sopping wet, the ground around me turning to muck.

"Whaa?" I spluttered, struggling to rise. Then my belly clenched painfully, and I collapsed. My body felt like it was on fire, and my chest was growing tighter, making breathing difficult. *Too* difficult. *What's happening to me?!*

"She needs more water!" I heard Mistflower's voice. It sounded distant. "Hurry!" Then another wave of water splashed onto me, and I relaxed.

Birch was standing above me, muzzle tight with worry. Mistflower stood at his side, terror in her eyes. Cynthia and Poppy huddled nearby, eyes round and scared.

Then I heard Sunshine, one of the Power-Holders, speaking. "The water should have cooled her down, but she might get too cold. Keep an eye on her fever."

"What's wrong with her?!" Mistflower practically shrieked.

"It must have been that blue flower." That was Oriole's voice. "Apparently it was bad to eat. But Delta should be fine in a few days."

They continued to talk, but exhaustion was drawing on my limbs, and I sank back into sleep, despite the fact that I was surrounded by water.

I didn't feel completely better for days, but, finally, I was able to return to training.

I'm never going to eat a flower again, even on accident! I thought as I padded toward the tunnel that led to the Training Cave.

"Delta!" Peak scampered up to walk beside me. "I'm so glad you're feeling better!"

I thought about ignoring him, but he was too nice for that. "Yeah. Today we'll be learning the chant for healing. They had to wait on me because I was sick."

"That's awesome!" Peak said enthusiastically. "About the chant, not you being sick!"

I laughed stiffly. "Well, I'd better go. See you around, Peak."

"Bye, Delta!" He called after me. "Good luck!"

I don't need luck. I hurried down the tunnel and into the Training Cave. All the young wolves sat around the platforms. Sunshine stood on it, and her eyes lit up as she saw me. "Young Delta! It's good to have you back."

"Thanks," I dipped my head, then took a spot next to Lemon. I noticed Sky was shooting me dirty looks, but I ignored her.

"We'll be learning the healing spell today," Sunshine called out, "That way if any of you become Power-Holders you will be able to use your Lostina."

She placed her paw on a jagged rock, and, with a terrible ripping noise, cut it deliberately. A ripple of shock passed through the crowd of young wolves, but Sunshine didn't seem in pain. "This cut is mild. I will have one of the other Power-Holders heal it later. That's something to remember – you cannot heal your own wounds, and there's a limit to how serious it can be. Now, who wants to try the chant first?" I flinched as her eyes fell on me. "Delta! You're a young, bright wolf. Why don't you?"

I felt frozen with fear, just as I had in front of the Guardian Stone. Then I stumbled forward to stand on the platform next to Sunshine. I realized how small I really was compared to the Power-Holder.

"But she's just a pup!" Sky rose to her paws with an angry huff. "She doesn't know anything!"

I opened my mouth to spit out a furious retort, but Sunshine stared back at the young she-wolf calmly. "You will not speak to a fellow Guardian like that, Sky. Apologize."

Sky plopped back to the ground, mumbling a muted and sulky apology.

"Now," Sunshine turned towards me, "you will place a paw on my injury when you want to heal it. Say these words – *broken skin, come together, may your wound be healed and whole."*

I nodded, and she held out her injured paw. I gulped, then placed a paw on it. A little blood leaked out, and I flinched. *I can't do this!*

Then I saw that Lemon was hopping up and down, encouragement in her eyes. *You've got this, Delta.* With a deep breath, I closed my eyes and recited the spell. "Broken skin, come together, may your wound be healed and whole."

When I opened my eyes, Sunshine's tail was wagging, but her paw was still injured. That made sense – I didn't *actually* have any power yet. "Well done, Delta," she said, her voice proud. "If you had the power, you would have just healed my paw." She whirled to face the group of young wolves. "Who's next?"

As I padded back through the tunnel, I thought about what I had done today. I'd watched, amused, as Sky forgot half the spell. Lemon had done well, which I was glad of. After class, Sunshine had told me that my chanting was the best.

"Come on, Delta!" Poppy bounced around me. Her lesson must have finished before mine. "We're going to choose where we want to sleep in the Sleeping Den!"

While I had been sick, we had become six moons old. My sisters had decided to wait for me, which I really appreciated.

"Okay!" I gave her a friendly nudge, nodding to Cynthia as she bounded up. "Let's go!"

The Sleeping Chamber was quiet, save the gentle snores of surrounding wolves. I knew I should get some sleep, but I was afraid of having another vision.

What was wrong with me? If any pup should have visions, it should be Poppy. I could hear her now, tossing and turning in her sleep, muttering softly.

She hadn't told any of us yet, but I could tell how stressful her lessons were. I assumed she still hadn't gotten her Lostina to work.

My dream kept creeping into my mind. The black she-wolf, which I recognized as Willow, had seemed so scared. What if I had the power to prevent a future catastrophe? But I still couldn't even think about telling Oriole, or any others.

Not even my sisters.

With a sigh, I rose to my paws and silently crept into the Crystal Cavern. There were no guards in sight.

Heaving another sigh, I crossed the water and peered into the Guardian Stone. My reflection shone back at me– a small pup with thick gray fur and ice-blue eyes.

Then another wolf's reflection joined mine. It was Peak.

I turned to face him. "You shouldn't be up this late."

His pale green eyes twinkled. "Neither should you."

I turned back to the Stone. "I just need time to think."

"About what?" Peak's voice was genuinely curious.

He was a friend. He wouldn't tell anyone if I asked him not to. Not even Cynthia and Poppy.

I took a deep breath. "I had a vision. Two, actually."

I expected him to burst into laughter, but his face only grew more curious. "What were they about?"

"In the first one, three Guardians sacrificed themselves to save a forest from a cloud of pulsating darkness," I began. It sounded even crazier out loud. "In the last one, the wolves were gone, and it was up to me to sacrifice myself to the darkness."

Peak's eyes flickered with something. Was that fear? "What do you think it means, Delta? It sounds terrifying!"

"I don't know," I admitted, "and I don't want any of the others to know. They might think I'm crazy."

"But this sounds important!" he insisted.

I gave him a hard stare. "It won't to wolves that would think I'm just a selfish pup trying to steal my sister's spotlight."

"Oh," Peak sighed, then glanced at me. "I'll keep it a secret, Delta. I promise. I'm your friend."

I gave his shoulder a grateful nudge. "Thank you, Peak. You really are a good friend. We'd better get back into the Sleeping Chamber before a guard comes around."

I began to pad back down the tunnel, and he followed. I was glad to have a friend I could trust.

7

The next morning I was trotting up the tunnel on my way to meet up with my sisters and Peak after a great lesson. I had answered lots of hard questions, and said the healing chant perfectly, with no hesitation this time.

I halted when I heard a distressed voice. That sounded like Poppy! I slipped into the dark branch-off the tunnel that led to where she would be training.

"You'll learn to control it eventually." That was Sunshine's voice.

"I'm finally able to use it!" Poppy's voice was scared. "And I hurt your paw even worse than the cut I was supposed to be healing!"

"You'll learn," Sunshine's voice was calm. "Don't worry, Poppy."

My sister's stomping paw steps began ascending my way. I quickly rushed up the tunnel and into the Crystal Cavern, where Cynthia and Peak were waiting.

"What's up, Delta?" Peak asked in concern as I halted, breathing hard.

"Nothing," I said quickly, "just wanting to hurry." I couldn't tell them what I had just heard. Poppy was getting discouraged. My heart reached out to my poor sister. I would do all I could to be nice to her from now on, and that meant not teasing her about Peak.

Poppy came trudging up behind me, head low.

"Do you want to hear a story from Fern?" Cynthia suggested. She met my eyes, worry for our sister in them. She was, after all, only six moons old.

"Sure!" Peak said cheerfully. Poppy just nodded slowly. They began padding over towards where the elder wolf was gossiping with a group of wolves.

"I'll be right there," I called after them, then padded back to the tunnel that led to the Training Cave. I was going to ask Sunshine how Poppy was doing. The Power-Holder was really nice. She would tell me.

But as I went down the tunnel, I heard Oriole's voice.

"How's young Poppy doing?"

"She's struggling." That was Sunshine. "I don't think she's strong enough to handle it, she's still so young! We should have waited to tell her what her future was, just like we're waiting to tell her sister."

My eyes widened. Poppy wasn't the only one with a unique destiny? Did Cynthia *really* have a special future? My heart beat faster. Was it *me?*

Not waiting to hear the rest of the conversation, I rushed back to the Crystal Cavern, wishing I hadn't heard what I just had.

If I was the other special pup, I would have to concentrate more on what I was learning. There would be no time for play.

Starting now, I was going to focus on my studies, and work harder.

"Why would you rather help me make beds than play with the other pups?" Mistflower asked suspiciously, as we reshaped the bracken beds in the Sleeping Chamber a few days later.

"Because," I answered my mother, "I can concentrate more on my studies here. We're learning the chant for shape-shifting soon. I need to be ready."

She sighed. "Delta, you are still a very young wolf. You don't need to study so hard. It's not like you're to be future leader!"

You don't understand. What if I am *to be future leader?* I couldn't say the words out loud.

I'd thought about what Oriole and Sunshine had said a few days ago, and now I was sure they had been talking about me. Cynthia didn't have a future with magic. I possibly did.

Mistflower nodded reluctantly as my silence stretched on. "Study, then." She left the Chamber, now that all the beds were done.

I plopped down in the center, closing my eyes. *Broken skin, come together, may your wound be healed and whole.* I was getting good at that! *Lostina dwells in every wolf, but only those with high amounts are able to use it. Vestina is a dark form of Lostina that plants itself in the hearts of wolves suffering anger, loss, envy, or hatred—*

"Delta!"

My eyes flew open. Peak stood there. "Hi."

"Hi," he said, kind of awkwardly. "I just wondered why you aren't playing with us."

"I need to study," I said dispassionately.

His tail twitched. "That's what you've been saying. What happened, Delta?"

My heart began to warm. He was so kind. Then my resolve hardened. I had to study! "I'm fine! I just want to be left alone."

His face twisted with hurt and shock at my harsh tone. "Sorry you feel that way." He turned and raced out of the Sleeping Chamber.

I ducked my head with guilt. Peak was my friend! Why had I just snapped at him?!

With a little whimper, I pushed him out of my mind. I had work to do.

...suffering anger, loss, envy, or hatred. It can fester in a wolf, slowly taking them over without them even realizing. It's a very dangerous form of darkness, and one must avoid it at all costs...

I found myself wondering if any past wolves had caved in to Vestina. I vowed then and there that no matter what happened, I would avoid it.

8

"Wow, Delta," Lemon commented one day as we padded away from the Training Cave, "how are you six moons old and already so smart?"

"Soon to be seven moons," I corrected her, "and I've just studied a lot."

"This isn't fair!"

We turned to see Sky storming towards us. "I'm an adult wolf! I should be top of the class, not some tiny pup!"

"Adult wolves don't act like that," Lemon snapped, "if *you* want to impress Oriole as much as Delta has, then I would suggest traveling to the Boglands and back!"

"Yeah!" I forced down a laugh. The Boglands was the swamp that lay near High Mountain. "I bet he'll make you a Power-Holder right away!"

Sky's face was furious. "I just might do that, pup!" She pushed past us, stomping away.

"What an overgrown pup!" Lemon huffed. "Come on, Delta, let's study together."

"All right," I agreed, watching Sky's black-furred form melt into the darkness of the tunnel up ahead. "Let's wait for Poppy, though. She may want to help."

"Not really." My copper-furred sister plodded out of the branch-off tunnel, "I'll probably embarrass myself."

Without waiting for an answer, she went on.

"Has anyone seen Sky? I haven't seen her all morning!"

The chunk of meat in my mouth plopped out.

A she-wolf with black fur had just raced into the Crystal Cavern. "I can't find my daughter anywhere!"

My eyes locked with Lemon's, where she sat a few feet away. Cynthia, Poppy, and Peak had also stopped eating.

"Has anyone seen Sky?" Oriole called from the base of the Guardian Stone. "If you know anything, speak!"

Commotion erupted, as every wolf began to speak at once, suggesting possibilities.

I crept to Lemon's side, my belly fluttering with unease. "She must have gone to the Boglands," I whispered, "we need to follow her!"

The blonde she-pup nodded. "Let's go."

Lemon and I quickly slipped into the tunnel that led to the surface. I felt a rush of fear as we emerged into the freezing air, remembering my near-death experience. What if that happened to Sky?

"How do we get down?" Lemon was shaking in the cold.

I lifted my nose, scenting wolf. That had to be Sky! Creeping to the edge of High Mountain's apex, I saw a trail of paw prints that led down a ledge that wasn't as steep as the others. "Let's go."

Placing one paw in front of the other, I began the downward climb.

"Good thing it isn't snowing," Lemon commented as we slid further down, watching for loose rocks, "or Sky's tracks would be gone."

"I don't know much about this stuff yet, but her trail smells a few hours old." I tried to keep my voice light. "She must have left really early this morning."

"Berry brain!" Lemon spat. "She should have realized we were teasing!"

"It's our fault, though," I said glumly. The mountain slope was getting steeper. I noticed that the paw prints in front of us changed. The depressions in the snow seemed like Sky had slid straight down the mountain. But why would she do that?

Suddenly the stone beneath our paws was very, very, *very* slick. With a screech of terror from both of us, we lost all footing.

Terror clawed at my chest as I found myself on my back, sliding endlessly down High Mountain. Snow piled up in my thick fur, weighing me down.

"Lemon!" I howled, losing sight of her blonde fur.

Then the solid substance that was the only thing between me and the ground was gone.

I let out a piercing scream of excruciating terror as I fell.

"Delta! Wake up!"

My eyes flew open. I was half-buried in a deep drift of snow on a ledge. Lemon's head was poking out of the snow a few feet away.

"We have to get out of this!" She whimpered. "It's so cold!"

I tried to move my legs, but my body seemed frozen, stuck inside the tightly-packed ice. "I don't think we can!" I cried. "It's too hard…" My brain was fuzzy, but I tried to remember what had happened.

Sky had gone missing… We were looking for her… We'd fallen down High Mountain. I had no idea *how* far down, though. If only we could escape the snow!

But we couldn't. Lemon's eyes were closing. Numbness reached into my flesh until I felt nothing. It would all be fine. We'd be fine. All we had to do was rest…

My head snapped up. *No! Sky needs us* now! I was special— I could fight!

With a squeal of pain, I wrenched a forepaw out of the snow. It was chapped and bloody, but I didn't care. I yanked another paw free, then used my forepaws to drag myself out of the snow. "Come on, Lemon!" I howled. "We're future Power-Holders! We've got this!"

Lemon groaned, then opened her eyes. "I can't."

"Then I'll help you!" I rammed my front paws onto the ice surrounding her, sending cracks across the surface. I felt a flicker of surprise that I, a pup of nearly seven moons old, was able to do that. Then I rammed the ice again, until my friend was able to break free.

Just like me, she was cut up, but they weren't serious wounds. I met her eyes, and she nodded shakily. "Thank you, Delta. Let's go."

We crept to the edge of the crag and peered over. The ground was not far beneath us. Lying in a grassy clearing at the edge of a forest was a dark shape.

"Sky!" I felt a shiver of dread. "She must have rolled down, right over the edge!" I then realized how lucky Lemon and I had been.

"Let's go!" Lemon slid down a little embankment at the edge of the small ledge that led down to the forest. I followed her, and we were on the ground before long. The frosted grass beneath our paws crunched as we took a few steps forward.

"The clearing should be over here." Lemon padded through a thick patch of trees, vanishing from view.

I began to follow her, then halted as screams racked my brain. They seemed to be coming from everywhere at once!

I saw the faint outlines of three wolves rush past, charging towards a black, pulsating mass that rose above the forest.

I shrank down to the ground, squeezing my eyes shut. When I opened them, the forest seemed normal once more.

"Delta! Hurry! She's hurt!"

Snapping out of my thoughts, I raced after Lemon, emerging into the clearing. The blonde-furred pup crouched at a black mass of fur that lay on the ground.

"Sky!" I peered at the she-wolf's face. It was covered in blood. "No, no, no! We need help!" I backed away from the wolf's broken form, horror rising like bile into my throat.

"Pups!" A deep, familiar voice called. "Where are you?"

"Oriole!" I sped back to the edge of the mountain, where several wolves were emerging from a cleverly concealed crack in the stone. A secret passage!

But my excitement over the discovery was drowned by fear for Sky. "We found Sky! She's hurt real badly!"

Oriole glanced back at the other wolves– the other nine Power-Holders. "Lead the way, Delta."

I raced back to where Lemon sat at Sky's side. "She fell off a cliff!"

"Both of you pups stay back," Sunshine commanded.

We did as we were told, watching as two of the Power-Holders lifted Sky and began carrying her to the secret tunnel.

I followed anxiously as they slowly carried her up, into the darkness. "Will she be okay?"

Oriole turned to me and Lemon, his expression grave. "I don't know."

We padded up the dark tunnel, emerging into the Crystal Cavern after what seemed to be forever. The tunnel was behind the waterfall.

The Guardians gathered around as Sky was placed beside the Guardian Stone.

Lemon ran to her parents, but I just sat there numbly. A cold snout touched my shoulder. Peak sat next to me, his green eyes comforting. I could tell he wanted to ask what had happened, but knew I didn't want to talk. Cynthia and Poppy joined us, and I suddenly didn't feel so alone.

9

I was older. Not just physically, but mentally as well. At least, it felt like it.

I sighed, watching as Sky padded across the Crystal Cavern, guided by her mother. The young she-wolf's face was torn up. She had lost her sense of sight, and now had quite a few scars.

Lemon and I were apparently "heroes" for saving her. But if it weren't for us, she would be okay.

"Delta!" Peak scampered up to sit by me. "Want to play with us?" He cocked his head. "Or are you too busy studying?"

I was about to refuse, then decided that spending time with them would be good. I followed Peak over to where Cynthia and Poppy sat chatting.

"Delta!" Cynthia's tail wagged as she saw us. "We were just talking about visions! I wonder if Poppy will ever have any!"

Poppy's ears flattened. "I hope not."

My focus went fuzzy as I remembered everything I had experienced since my first encounter with the Guardian Stone.

*Tell them…*A voice breathed in my ear.

I wavered, my senses rippling between the present and a dream. Could I tell them about the vision? *Should* I tell them? A terrible feeling told me that I should, but my stubborn side refused to let me speak of it—I could be laughed at, or even seem to be trying to take Poppy's spotlight. I couldn't. It was nothing but the imagination of a pup.

I shook my head, seeing clearly once more. The conversation had moved on.

Now they were talking about Sky. "I feel really bad for her," Peak commented.

"Yes," Cynthia said softly, "she won't be a Power-Holder in training now."

Guilt flooded my veins. It was unbearable. "I thought we were going to play something, not sit around and talk!"

Peak lowered his head, but his eyes were thoughtful. "You're right, Delta."

"Let's play wrestle!" Poppy howled, just as eager as I was to get away from all our troubles.

Later in the day I didn't feel like talking to any wolves, so I just sat at the edge of the Crystal Cavern, near the waterfall, watching the Guardians chat. Even Sky seemed happy. There was no worry to be seen.

Except for in me. How could I have a special future after *this?*

That was just it. I couldn't. I was a disaster waiting to happen, the reason a fellow Guardian had been permanently injured! There was no way I deserved a unique destiny—there was no way I deserved to be a Guardian.

No wolves were watching me. Without a backward glance, I padded behind the waterfall.

The dark tunnel loomed, its gaping jaws wide, the rocky ground vanishing downward. I whooshed out a breath, then trotted into the blackness.

Every breath seemed to echo off the damp, mossy walls. *Is this right? Should I leave? I'm just a pup! It's dangerous!* All those thoughts flew through my head, but with each one I grew more determined to leave.

My paw steps, once uncertain, now drummed on rhythmically. I continued to put each paw in front of the other, staring straight ahead into the darkness.

Fifty steps. A hundred steps.

I stopped counting after two hundred. The small passage had never felt *this* suffocating before.

After what seemed to be forever, I emerged out of the passageway and into the open.

The forest was alive. Birds sang as they welcomed the unexpected sunny weather. The grass was soft beneath my leathery paw pads.

My belly growled. I'd never *really* learned how to hunt, but I would try. I was too small to catch a rabbit, much less a deer, but a mouse would work.

My ears picked up the sound of tiny scrabbling paws.

There.

Dropping down, I watched as the little creature skittered from one tree. I lunged for it with a high-pitched howl.

It tried to turn around, but my paws ended its life immediately.

I felt weird as I looked down at my prey. I had never had to kill anything before to survive.

I shook my head. I was being silly! I ate this stuff all the time!

As I munched on my meal, I felt a tug of anxiety. The sun was setting, and I had nowhere to sleep. I might have gotten lucky with the mouse, but what if that was all I could find?

The forest suddenly seemed very dark. Shadows seemed to reach out towards me, and eyes seemed to blink from the treetops. My fur bushed out. What if I ran into a cougar? I had heard Fern tell about how she'd run into some before coming to the Guardians. They were huge, with long, wiry bodies and a snaking tail. Not to mention the razor-sharp claws.

I scratched a small depression into the moss underneath one of the less-suspicious trees, then settled into it, curled into a tight ball.

If only I hadn't left! *But I had to. I no longer belong with the Guardians.*

I let out a small whine at that thought. I could go back, live normally. Surely Sky would understand that I hadn't meant to cause such trouble?

But I'd made a choice.

I couldn't go back on it.

I tried to block out the sounds of the forest, knowing that it would be a long, sleepless night, filled with nightmares and darkness.

10

I didn't figure I would sleep much that night. When I awoke, I was still alive (at first I had thought I'd been eaten and was now a ghost, but that was before I tripped over a tree root and landed on my snout).

I tried to be quiet as I searched for prey, but there were just so many brittle twigs to step on. If only I could do that shapeshifting thing that Oriole did. I could catch anything!

Just the thought of the Guardian leader made me want to go home so badly! But if I did, I would have to explain why I had left. I couldn't do that.

The day waned on, with me searching fruitlessly for something, *anything* to eat. I found a small creek, eagerly drinking my fill. My belly growled, and I knew I would have to find something tomorrow.

I made a small depression in the soft dirt next to the water, preparing for the next day—the second day I would be alone.

I continued to search for prey the following day.

My paws were growing heavy, plodding along noisily, scaring away anything within a mile radius. Despair filled my chest, and my empty stomach growled.

Finally, exhausted and hungry, I scanned my surroundings. The forest was giving way to wet, marshy ground. I was near the Boglands.

Have I really travelled this far? I thought bleakly. By tomorrow I could be in a land I had never even heard of before.

The Boglands were beautiful. I liked it better than the forest. There weren't as many trees, and the cool water quenched my thirst. It couldn't beat a mountain, though.

With a sigh, I plopped down next to a clear lake. A ledge rose up over my head, jutting out over the water. This would be a nice place to live.

My dreams were filled with howls of terror. They were looking for me, but I wasn't there for them! Darkness was descending on the world, a pulsating wall of destruction and death.

And in the center of it all… Peak was howling and yipping in pain, his green eyes stretched wide in desperation.

The Guardians were gone.

My eyes flew open. I was gasping for breath beside the small lake.

The Boglands were silent.

"Delta!"

My fur bushed out as I heard the familiar voice. *Peak?*

The gray-furred pup emerged from some bracken. "I saw you leave. I followed you."

I felt a rush of annoyance. Why did he always have to care so much? "I wanted to leave."

"Why?" His voice was genuinely curious.

"It's my fault Sky got hurt!" I burst out. The weight on my chest lightened, so I went on. "Lemon and I told her that if she travelled all the way to the Boglands – here – and back, Oriole would be so impressed that he'd make her a Power-Holder. We were so stupid! Now she's lost all hope of ever being a Power-Holder." I dropped my gaze to my paws. There. Now he knew. He'd turn around and return to High Mountain. I risked a glance upward.

Peak's eyes were wide, but he said nothing.

I flattened my ears. "Don't you see? It's *my* fault! I don't deserve to be a Guardian!" I meant those words with every fiber of my being, but a deep, desperate longing inside wanted Peak to tell me I was wrong, that I *did* have a place in the Guardians.

My friend's eyes were soft. "Delta, you may have played a part in Sky's accident, but she shouldn't have taken you so literally. She's a full-grown wolf. She should have known better. Delta, please. Come back."

I turned away from him, squeezing my eyes shut. A battle was waging in my mind. My shame told me to just walk away, and find a new life—but my honor told me to return, and face the Guardians. I knew which one to listen to, though it wasn't easy. "I'll go." It was hard admitting it, but he was right. I had to own *my* part of what had happened, not *all* of it.

Peak was at my side in an instant. "Thank you, Delta. You're a great friend."

"So are you," I faced him, trying with all my might to keep my will from wavering. I had to be strong. "Let's go."

I felt a twinge of terror as Peak and I stopped at the end of the secret tunnel, right behind the waterfall. What would I say to explain myself? It had been days since I'd left!

A snout touched my shoulder. "Follow my lead," Peak whispered. Then he marched into the Crystal Cavern.

I found myself forging another mental battle, my paws frozen.

I slunk after him, wincing as all eyes fell on me.

"Delta!" Mistflower and Birch rushed up to me, followed by my sisters. "Why did you leave?" My mother's voice was outraged. "There can't be any explanation for why you did that!"

Oriole padded up, followed by the other nine Power-Holders. The Guardians all crowded around.

I gulped.

"Delta was super upset about Sky's accident!" Peak spoke up, looking at the Guardian leader earnestly. "She feels that she and Lemon didn't get there fast enough!"

My head snapped up, and I stared at him, wondering what in the world he was thinking.

I saw Lemon look away, her eyes upset. I wondered why Sky wasn't saying anything. She knew that I was partly responsible for her blindness. I'd think she'd want revenge!

Oriole's eyes held sympathy. "Delta, you shouldn't have run away. But I understand."

I squirmed, opening my jaws. A feeling deep inside whispered to me that Peak was wrong. He shouldn't lie. Then my jaws slowly closed. I was too afraid.

He turned to Peak. "And *you* should have told us instead of following her."

Peak's head dropped. "Forgive us, Oriole."

The Guardian leader nodded. "Of course. But you should be focusing on your futures, not your pasts. That is what we do as Guardians."

"Yes, Oriole," I dipped my head to him, voice slightly choked. I no longer felt overwhelmed by guilt about Sky, but now I had a new reason to feel guilty—Peak had just lied to our leader.

And I had let him.

I sat still in the Crystal Cavern, head drooping. My parents had tried to cheer me up with some fresh meat, but I wasn't in the mood.

My insides were roiling, and I felt like throwing up. Peak—my *best* friend, who I trusted—had lied to the leader of the Guardians.

For me.

The horrible feeling in my stomach grew. He'd been trying to help me, but I knew deep inside that he had gone about it in a terrible way.

I had to tell Oriole.

I had to say how I felt—that I had run away because of the guilt I felt over Sky.

And why I felt it.

But I was so scared.

I wasn't strong enough.

I had to be.

I couldn't do it.

"Delta?" Mistflower nuzzled my ear. "Are you alright, Daughter?"

I snapped my eyes up toward her. "Yeah. I'm good."

I could tell she didn't believe me.

I didn't believe myself.

A pup shouldn't have to feel this way.

But I did.

11

"Sure you want to go over alone, Delta?" Lemon nudged my shoulder softly.

I nodded firmly. "I know what I have to say."

Sky was sitting beside her mother in the Crystal Cavern. Though nervousness tugged at me, I forced myself to pad over. "Hello."

Sky looked up sharply, scenting me. Her scarred muzzle lifted slightly.

"Delta," her mother nodded at me, "I don't blame you for what happened, even when you didn't get there in time. You saved my daughter's life. That's all that matters."

It was all I could do to keep myself from crumbling to the floor in shame. "Can I talk to Sky?"

The she-wolf stood. "Of course. I'll go grab some prey." She padded off.

I sat down, feeling awkward. "Sky, I'm sorry."

"Really?" The black wolf's voice was scathing. *"Really!* It's your fault I'm blind."

"Not fully," I winced as she bristled, then hurried on, "though I had a part to play in it. I own that."

Sky seemed suspicious of my sincere apology. "I may not be able to fully forgive you now, pup, but maybe someday."

"One more thing." I leaned forward curiously. "Why didn't you speak up the other day?"

The black she-wolf shrugged. "I don't know, really. But you heard what Oriole said. It's time to look to the future."

Sky's mother came back at that moment, carrying a rabbit. I nodded at her. "Thanks for letting me chat with Sky."

She dropped the prey. "Of course, young one."

"Goodbye, Sky," I said quietly, but she didn't answer. I hurried off to where Lemon waited.

"Delta," she whispered, "what did she say? Does she want revenge?"

I shook my head. "No."

The blonde she-pup sighed in relief. "Good. Now everything is fine, except for the fact that your friend lied."

My eyes dropped. "Yeah. But it'll be okay. We're looking to the future now."

Though I said those words, my head swirled with doubts and guilt.

"Fur to feathers, scales to skin! Change me on the outside, but not from within!"

"Excellent demonstration, Delta," Sunshine's voice held pride, "if you had power, you would have just shapeshifted. You may be only seven moons old, but you've quickly risen to top of this group."

My chest swelled with pride. "Thank you." I padded back into the crowd of young wolves, wagging my bushy tail as they gave me friendly nudges.

"Wow, Delta!" Lemon's eyes were excited. "You're *so* good at this! I bet Oriole chooses to make you a Power-Holder!" She lowered her voice, leaning closer. "Maybe even future leader."

My mind shot back to when I'd overheard what Oriole had said. Was that true? Had the Guardian Stone chosen *me* as leader? Was that why I had terrifying dreams? Or was all of this just a coincidence? I winced inwardly. Oriole would probably want to know about the dreams. But I might be completely wrong about them being visions!

"You are all growing so quickly." Sunshine looked over us, eyes finally resting on me. "I believe that even if you are not chosen to be a Power-Holder, you will still have a special part to play in the Guardians."

I barely heard what she said next. I was distracted by a strange buzzing in my ears. My vision grew fuzzy, just as it had before. *Delta…* A voice spoke, seeming to come from everywhere at once. *Delta… Oriole must know… You must tell him, before it's too late…*

My focus returned. My mouth was suddenly dry. What did the voice want me to tell Oriole about? My heart skipped a beat suddenly. Of course. It meant that I should tell him the truth, that Sky's accident was not completely her fault.

And I wanted to, so badly, but I was too afraid! What if he banished me? A Guardian was rarely banished. Was what I'd done bad enough? What if I had returned just to leave again?

I was too afraid.

I was a coward.

At that moment a loud *bang* echoed through the mountain. The rock beneath my paws shook as if it were shifting. Terror shot through me.

Some of the younger wolves erupted into howls of fear. I felt like doing the same, but then Sunshine bounded over to me and Lemon.

"It's a storm!" She tried calling above the din of new thundering, but they drowned out all sounds. She whirled to face me. "Delta! Lemon! Try to calm some of them down!"

I nodded, then raced into the mob of terrified wolves. I let out a squeak of pain as one of my paws was pounded on, falling to the ground. They were going to crush me!

Dust rained down from the ceiling as thunder shook the mountain. Gritting my teeth, I rose painfully, then leaped on top of a nearby white pup.

He stared up at me, eyes huge. "We're going to die!"

"No! We aren't!" I had to yell at him over all the noise. "It's just a storm!" My pelt pricked with worry, though. Could a storm this big destroy our home within the mountain? I returned my focus to the pup. "What is your name?"

He seemed to be trying really hard to stay calm. "Boulder."

I stepped off him. "Don't worry, Boulder. Sunshine's got this all under control."

His eyes moved upward. "Boulder!"

"Yeah, you already told me." I began to wonder if this wolf was wrong in the head.

"BOULDER!" He shrieked, pointing his muzzle up.

My gaze darted upward, and my mouth went dry. A huge *boulder* was breaking free of the ceiling.

It was directly above me.

With a howl of terror, I started to leap out of the way, but my injured paw gave out, and I collapsed to the ground. The rock fell.

At that moment Boulder the pup snatched my scruff in his jaws, dragging me out of the way with a tug. The rock hit the ground, inches away from the tip of my tail. Dust from the impact filled the air, making me sneeze.

By now many of the Power-Holders in training had left the Training Cave. The storm raged on, but there wasn't as much thunder anymore.

I scrambled to my paws, careful not to put any weight on the injured one. "Boulder! You saved me from the boulder!"

He shrugged, still looking a bit nervous at the storm. "It was nothing. My name is still Boulder, by the way."

"Everyone get out of here *now!*" Sunshine shrieked. "The ceiling's caving in!"

I rushed for the tunnel, but my injured paw slowed me down. The ceiling was cracking!

Then Lemon pushed her shoulder into me, helping me stand. Boulder took my other side, and we hurried to get out of the doomed Training Cave.

Luckily we were the last wolves in there, because rocks smashed down, sealing off the tunnel behind us.

"To the Crystal Cavern!" Boulder said, and we followed all the other terrified Guardians, as the storm's noise rose to a horrible pitch.

"Delta!" Peak raced up to me, followed by Cynthia and Poppy. "You're okay!"

"Yes, thanks to Lemon and Boulder," I replied.

"Are all the Guardians safe?" A voice shouted over all the noise. Oriole stood at the base of the Guardian Stone. His dark red coat was dulled by dust, but he held himself tall. At that moment I was so thankful that we had such a fearless leader.

"Sky was outside!" A voice shrieked. Her mother was trembling. "She was going to get some fresh air. I told her not to get near the edge of the mountain, but the rain and wind will sweep her off!"

Determination settled inside me. I was going to save the wolf I'd almost killed.

I broke free of Lemon and Boulder's support, though it hurt really bad setting my paw down. "I'm going to save her."

"Then we're going with you, Delta," Peak stepped forward, "even to death." The others nodded.

I nodded, and my tail wagged slightly. "Come on." We were near the tunnel that led to the peak of High Mountain, so we just slipped inside.

Water ran down the tunnel floor, making it slippery. I felt a flash of worry. What if our home flooded?

"This is going to be hard!" Lemon called out. A flash of lightning illuminated the darkness, showing my friends' terrified expressions.

"We have to save Sky!" Cynthia was at my side, half-pushing me upwards.

I winced in pain as my paw throbbed. "You're right, Sister."

Then we were out in the full heat of the storm. The wind screamed, trying to rip our paws out from underneath us. The snow had melted, and now all ground was covered by a flood of icy water that was dragging everything it could right off the side of the mountain. Thunder cracked, making us all jump.

"Help!"

My head jerked in the direction of the noise. "Sky! Where are you?"

"About to lose my grip on a rock, that's where I am!"

I spotted the black she-wolf clinging to a large rock, the water tugging at her violently. The mountain's edge was right behind her. If she lost her grip…

"We're coming, Sky!" I whirled to face the other pups. "Peak, Cynthia! Come with me to go get Sky! Boulder, Lemon, be ready to grab any of us if we lose our footing! Poppy, go get Oriole!"

My copper-furred sister nodded, eyes huge, then raced back down the tunnel. I was glad she was out of immediate danger, at least.

Boulder and Lemon watched fearfully as Cynthia, Peak, and I waded carefully towards where Sky held on for dear life. Fear pounded in my chest, nearly drowning out the noise of the storm, but I was determined to save Sky!

"Delta, look out!" Peak called sharply.

I quickly hopped out of the way as a slab of ice flowed past, nearly losing my footing because of my paw. "Thanks, Peak!"

We were so close to Sky now, but I didn't think she could hold on for much longer. She let out a howl of fear as the water splashed over her hindquarters. It was rising up to her chest— she was sinking deeper! Her blind eyes were wide with terror. She somehow knew that she was about to go over the edge.

"We're almost there!" I forced myself to go faster. The icy water swirled around my paws, reaching my belly. Why did I have to be a pup?!

I stood beside the rock now. Bracing myself against it, I stretched out my neck to grab Sky's scruff.

Then she slid underwater.

"NO!" I plunged myself down, desperately searching for her. My paws hit something soft, and I grabbed her scruff with my teeth.

But I couldn't fight the current *and* hold the weight of an adult wolf. I lost my footing, losing all sense of direction as well.

I was going to die!

Then teeth closed around *my* scruff. I was being pulled to the surface.

Still holding on tightly to Sky with my teeth, I looked up at my rescuer. Peak nodded at me. Cynthia stood right next to him. "You owe me now, Delta!" His eyes twinkled with a laugh.

"Pups!" Oriole's booming voice carried over to us. He stood next to Lemon and Boulder. Poppy was there as well. "Come over here *now!*"

I nodded to Peak and Cynthia, and they took Sky, carrying her limp form between them. Somehow I found the strength to wade after them. Oriole's muzzle was not tight with anger, as I'd expected.

"Pups!" He gasped out, staring at all of us, then at the limp black she-wolf. "You saved Sky!" Then he motioned with his muzzle at the tunnel. "Hurry! All of you get down there! I have to seal the entrance before our home is flooded!"

We all rushed to obey, with Lemon and Boulder helping me once more. As we hurried downwards, I glanced over my shoulder. Oriole was chanting something, and a wall of some solid substance covered the entrance.

Water was no longer flowing in, but the damage had already been done. The ground was really slippery, and any places that were made out of dirt or anything other than rock were muddy. The clear pond was a brown color, and the waterfall spewed debris into the water. The Training Room probably was not the only chamber destroyed.

Our home was a mess.

Oriole came up behind us, and I could see a troubled look in his eyes. He was thinking the same thing I was—the storm was worse than any I could ever remember. Had it been natural? Or had something caused it?

12

High Mountain was a wreck. Our tunnels and chambers were in pretty bad shape, and at least one other chamber was destroyed beside the Training Cave.

But the peak of the mountain was the worst. Snow was building up slowly, but it still could not hide the torn-up rock and various pools of water.

My pelt burned with irritation as I watched all the wolves in the Crystal Cavern trying to clean up. Oriole, as well as Mistflower and Birch, had forbidden me from doing any work, because I apparently needed to "rest my hurt paw" as they put it.

The thought of Sky and near-death experience made me somewhat more cheerful. I had been able to help save her. That mattered. Her mother and father had thanked all of us profusely. The blind she-wolf was now resting in the Sleeping Chamber.

Oriole had thanked us in front of all the Guardians. It had been *so* embarrassing, but also nice.

Cynthia, Poppy, Peak, Lemon, Boulder, and I had just done our part for the Guardians by reaching Sky in time.

I felt a slight sense of foreboding, though. The Guardian leader had been worried about the freak storm. It *had* been sudden.

A little *too* sudden.

What if it hadn't been normal?

"Delta." Peak crossed an arch to where I sat underneath the Guardian Stone. "I just wanted to say thanks for your leadership skills yesterday."

"We all saved Sky." I pointed out, feeling a rush of embarrassment. "That's why she still lives."

"No," Peak nudged my shoulder, "she's alive because of *your* determination. You know, you'd make a good leader."

I ducked my head. "Thanks, Peak."

"Well, I'd better get back to cleaning rubble," the gray-furred pup bounded away.

I thought about what he'd said. I *would* make a good leader. But I knew the toll it could have on wolves. Oriole was always so tired. Speaking of Oriole…

"Young Delta." the Guardian leader padded up to sit next to me, as if he had somehow sensed my thoughts. "You performed well the other night. Sky would have died if it wasn't for you and the others."

"We all worked together," I said quickly, but he shook his head.

"The other pups told me how you took charge, knowing just what to do. Then you nearly died trying to save Sky."

My chest swelled with pride at my leader's words. "Thank you, Oriole."

"We are proud to have you in the Guardians," the red-furred wolf rumbled, "and I think everyone knows you have a special future." His voice suddenly grew less firm. "Why, then, did you *truly* run away?"

My mind shot back to the reason. My belly churned. How could I tell him that I'd played a part in Sky's blindness? But I had to. I dropped my eyes to my paws. "Lemon and I told Sky that if she travelled to the Boglands and back, you'd be so impressed that you'd make her a Power-Holder right away. So, I had a part to play in her accident." A weight seemed to lift off my chest.

I waited fearfully for him to speak. Finally, he did. "Delta, you made a mistake, but you've owned that. I'd rather have Guardians that owned their shortcomings than try to hide them." His voice was kind. There was no trace of anger. "You may be somewhat responsible for Sky's blindness, but you are also chiefly responsible for saving her. You're a good pup, Delta, and you will grow into a good wolf."

I felt a rush of joy and pride. The Guardian leader believed in me. I could believe in myself.

"One more thing, young pup," he turned to me. "I should have done this earlier, but there was little time." He placed his paw over my injured one. "Broken skin, come together, may your wound be healed and whole."

The pain in my paw vanished. I carefully stood, putting weight on it. "Thank you, Leader!"

He chuckled at my enthusiasm. "We will need your determination if we are going to clean up this place."

I settled into my bed that night, exhausted but happy. With all the Guardians helping, we'd cleaned up nearly everything. There was nothing we could do for the collapsed chambers, though. Luckily no wolves had been caught in them!

Lemon and I followed the other young wolves as Stone– one of the Power-Holders– led us towards a new chamber that would become the new Training Cave.

It wasn't nearly as big as the old one, and it didn't have a stone platform, but it would do. Lemon and I quickly sat down near the front.

"You have all learned so much," Stone gazed out over us, "but only eight of you can continue to train as Power-Holders. You will be tested, and those that do the best will learn further. Not all of you are going to make it, but you are still Guardians, and can still use your knowledge."

We all nodded. I felt a twinge of fear.

"But aren't there ten Power-Holders?" Lemon called. "Why are you only choosing eight of us?"

"Because one of those ten is Poppy, the other is the leader," Stone replied, "and that is not our choice to make. A prophecy is always sent to determine the next leader. Now, let's begin."

My fear turned to horror. How could I compete with the older pups?! Obviously Stone thought I was ready. Poppy was *so* lucky! She didn't have to pass any tests!

"Reed, I will begin with you." Stone nodded at the young gray male wolf with white flecks in his fur. "Follow me to the Testing Chamber. The rest of you – stay here." Reed was literally shaking with fear as he followed Stone out of the Training Cave.

"I'm *so* nervous!" Lemon said as soon as they had left. "I'll make my parents so proud if I make it!"

I felt too sick to reply. I was going over every single thing I had ever learned. I couldn't, *wouldn't,* flunk this test!

Stone soon returned, but Reed was no longer with him. He chose another wolf, then left again.

As the hours ticked by, he kept returning for the next wolf, though none of the ones he had taken with him returned. Had they passed? Had they failed?

I managed to calm my nerves just enough to wish Boulder good luck as his turn came. Then I once more continued to review everything.

When Stone came back for a brown-and-white she-pup, I gave her an encouraging nod, because I could tell she was frozen with fear. She blinked at me before following the Power-Holder.

By now there were only three wolves left: me, Lemon, and a white male pup. Stone soon came to take him, then only Lemon and I remained.

"Are you scared, Delta?" Lemon asked me. Her eyes were fearful. "I am."

"Me too," I admitted, "but I know that I'll do my best."

"Right." Lemon began pacing, now that there was room to do so. "I wonder if you're told whether you've passed or not? Or maybe Oriole announces it!"

"That would be *so* embarrassing," I giggled, imagining it.

Suddenly Lemon whirled to face me. "Delta, even if one of us passes and the other doesn't, can we still be friends?"

"Of course!" I nudged her shoulder with my snout. "Always."

Then Stone entered the Training Room. "Lemon, are you ready?"

The blonde-furred she-pup faced him. "Yes."

"Good." He turned and vanished back down the tunnel.

"Go on," I told Lemon as she hesitated, "you'll do fine."

She nodded, then raced out of sight.

I wished suddenly that I did not have to be the last wolf tested. Now there was no one for me to talk to!

Now *I* began pacing, wishing I were anywhere but in this empty chamber. I was going to flunk! I was sure of it.

It seemed like hours before Stone padded into the Training Room. "Delta, are you ready?"

I faced him, taking a deep breath. "Yes."

"Then let's go." He padded down the tunnel.

I raced after him as we went into a branch-off tunnel that led downwards. My paw steps echoed strangely as I followed Stone into a tiny chamber.

My limbs froze as I saw that *all* the Power-Holders were here, including Oriole. They sat along the walls, fur shining. Stone joined them.

I was going to be tested in front of all ten Power-Holders.

"Delta," Oriole's voice echoed just as my paw steps had, "now is your time to show us that you have learned from us, and whether you are ready to move onto the next level."

"Why are you a Guardian?" Root, the russet Power-Holder, asked.

I hesitated. Was this a trick question? "Because..." Fear swirled in my mind. I was panicking. Then I shook my head. *Get a hold of yourself, Delta.* "Because I want to protect the light. I want to fight all forms of evil. I want to take care of the wolves I love."

Oriole's eyes were pleased, but he didn't say anything. Ripple, a pale-furred Power-Holder, spoke. "What is Lostina?"

This one was easy. "Lostina is what dwells in every wolf. It connects us. Wolves with more powerful Lostina are able to use it for good. But if darkness creeps into a wolf's mind, the Lostina becomes Vestina, a corrupted type of power."

"What is the chant for healing?" Sunshine asked.

"Broken skin, come together, may your wound be healed and whole," I replied.

"What about the chant for shapeshifting?" Stone gazed at me inquiringly.

"Fur to feathers, scales to skin," I recited, "change me on the outside, but not from within."

"Why do we live in High Mountain?" Dandelion, a black Power-Holder, asked.

"Because this is where the Guardian Stone rests," I replied, "and it's a perfect location, sheltered from any hostile creatures."

"You have done well, Delta," another Power-Holder, Pebble, rumbled.

"You have already proved yourself by saving Sky," Sand, another one, said, "your bravery is unquestionable, though you are but a pup."

"And your loyalty is strong," Wisp, a pale grey wolf, praised me.

Oriole stood. "Delta, you may go join the others in the Crystal Cavern. We will announce who has passed."

"Yes, Leader." I dipped my head to him, then calmly padded out of the chamber. As soon as I was in the tunnel, though, I raced as fast as I could to reach the Crystal Cavern. The Power-Holders had praised *me!* They thought *I* was loyal and brave!

All the Guardians were gathered when I emerged. I spotted Peak and Cynthia, but decided to go sit with the rest of the Power-Holders in training. Poppy was there as well.

"Delta," she nudged my shoulder, "how did you do?"

"Great!" I said softly, so only she could hear. "The Power-Holders said lots of great things about me."

Her brown eyes grew sad. "I feel guilty that I didn't have to take the test."

"Don't!" I replied. "It wasn't *too* hard."

"I bet you passed, Delta," Lemon came to sit with us, "I'm sure I didn't!"

"We're about to find out," I said, as Oriole and the other Power-Holders crossed the water and stood at the base of the Guardian Stone.

"Guardians!" Oriole howled. "Our young wolves have all tested to see if they are ready to move into deeper training! Only eight have passed, though, and have become our future Power-Holders! Of course, Poppy, a very special pup, will also be joining them! Poppy, come to the Stone!"

My sister gave me one scared glance, then padded through the throng of cheering wolves to join Oriole.

"Poppy," the Guardian leader looked at her kindly, "you are very special, gifted with strong Lostina. Your heart is big, and you care about helping those that need it. You will make a good Power-Holder someday."

Poppy dipped her head. "Thanks," she mumbled.

"Now," Oriole's gaze landed on me and the others, "I will call forward those that have been chosen. Boulder, come forward."

The white-furred pup gave a start, his eyes huge with shock. I gave him a nudge forward, and he stumbled up to stand next to Poppy.

"Boulder," Oriole said, "you have a caring heart as well. You are cautious, but not afraid to face danger when the need arises. You will make a good Power-Holder." He turned back to us. "Ruby!"

A dark red she-pup marched boldly up to the platform.

"You are a fierce wolf," Oriole said, "and are not afraid to speak your opinion. You will make a good Power-Holder." He once more turned to us. "Goldenrod!"

A she-pup with startlingly golden fur trotted up eagerly.

"You are always excited to learn," Oriole praised her, "and will spread that knowledge to others. You will make a good Power-Holder. Dewdrop!"

A small gray male pup shyly padded up to the Guardian Stone.

"You are always willing to make peace with others," Oriole said, "even if you get the low end. You will make a good Power-Holder. Lemon!"

Lemon whirled to face me, her jaw hanging open. I stifled a laugh, giving her a small push toward the others. She practically ran over the water and to Oriole.

"You are an excellent student," the leader gazed down at her, "and you always stand up for others. You will make a good Power-Holder. Reed!"

The gray male pup with white flecks in his fur excitedly joined the other young wolves that had passed.

"You have an affinity for remembering things," Oriole said, "and if any of your fellow students are in need, they come to you. You will make a good Power-Holder. Elderberry!"

A brown she-pup calmly padded up to him.

"You always keep a cool head," Oriole praised her, "even in difficult situations. You will make a good Power-Holder. And now, for the last one…"

I noticed the brown-and-white she-pup, Sunflower, squeeze her eyes shut, her tail wagging hopefully.

"Delta!"

My head shot up, and my eyes widened. Sunflower sighed in disappointment, and I gave her an apologetic look. Then I darted through the crowd of wolves and over an arch to stand with the others.

"You are brave and headstrong," Oriole turned to face me, "and you are good at taking charge. You will make a good Power-Holder!"

"What about our future leader?" A wolf howled.

Oriole faced the Guardians once more. "Now is not the time to announce that, even if the Stone *has* given me a vision. For now, these nine wolves will learn how to fit into their future roles."

13

I felt stunned. I was really going to be a Power-Holder someday.

The other chosen pups were talking together, including Poppy. I was about to join them, but then a muzzle touched my shoulder.

"Young Delta, are you prepared for the next stage of your training?" Oriole looked down at me kindly.

"Yes." I bowed my head to him. "I just wish the Guardian Stone would send you a vision of the future leader, though."

The Guardian leader nodded slowly. "One day all will be revealed, Delta. I would like you to watch me and the other Power-Holders replenish our power tonight."

"What?" I stared at him. "*Replenish* it?"

Oriole's graying muzzle crinkled as he laughed. "Yes, young one. We were given our power. It must be replenished every moon. We do it late at night, when all the other wolves are asleep."

"Of course I want to watch!" I bounced on my paws in excitement, then glanced backwards at my copper-furred sister. "Poppy has power. Why doesn't she have to do this?"

Oriole chuckled. "She was born with it, not given it."

"Can she watch, too?" I asked.

He shook his head. "I am only allowing you to watch because of what a good student you are."

"Oh." I nodded slowly, though I felt slightly guilty that my sister wouldn't be able to watch. What was so special about me that I was the only Power-Holder in training to see this?

Mistflower and Birch had been excited that the Power-Holders wanted me to watch the ceremony late tonight. Poppy and Cynthia didn't know, or else they would be upset, of course.

"This is a great honor," my mother had said earlier, when I had told her. "I hope you learn much from it, Delta."

I padded from the Sleeping Chamber, careful not to wake up any sleeping wolves. There were a few guards, but they let me pass into the Crystal Cavern, where the ten Power-Holders, including Oriole, waited at the base of the Guardian Stone.

I sat at the edge of the water, waiting.

The Power-Holders all lifted their heads to look at the very top of the Stone. They began speaking. "The power we hold must be restored, our Lostina brought back to its height. We commit to helping wolves of the world, and we commit to growing the light."

Their pelts began to glow, as well as their eyes. I could feel a powerful energy building in the air. It made me feel giddy and excited, like I had all the power of light within me.

But then the sensation was gone, and the Power-Holders were crossing the water.

"You should return to the Sleeping Chamber, Delta." Sunshine stopped to nod at me. "Remember what you saw tonight. You will someday participate."

"But I didn't just *see* it," I exclaimed, wagging my tail, "I *felt* it."

She gave me a thoughtful look, then followed the other Power-Holders as they headed to a tunnel. I noticed that Oriole went a different way. The leader must have his own chamber.

I slowly padded back to the Sleeping Chamber. I still felt a slight change in the air. It was strange.

But everything was strange these days.

I yawned, watching as wolves milled about the Crystal Cavern. I had not slept very well. I'd been bothered by another bad dream, just like the last. I felt a prickle in my conscience. I should have told Oriole long ago. Part of me wished Peak would tell some wolf, but I knew he wouldn't.

I couldn't say anything, because it would make me look like I was trying to steal Poppy's spotlight.

Today's lesson the eight Power-Holders in training (including me) had been taught (by Sunshine) was super exhausting (Poppy had private lessons, still). We had started going over some battle moves, just in case we would ever have to fight. I had done terribly, of course.

It didn't help that our surroundings were unfamiliar—we were in a new, larger, cave.

I stiffened as I saw the Guardian leader padding over to where I sat. Had he heard of how bad I had done? Was I going to be kicked out?

"Young Delta," Oriole peered down at me over his graying muzzle, "I must discuss something with you."

"I'm sorry about my fighting skills," I blurted out, "I know I am terrible!"

He chuckled. "You will learn, but no, that is not why I came over. I saw you go speak to Sky a while ago. I assume you were apologizing?"

"Yes," I said, wondering why he'd think I'd want to talk about this.

"That was a good thing to do," Oriole said, "and I hope you have forgiven yourself."

"Of course," I replied, "I'm going to do better. I'll be the best Guardian I can be, and never make any more mistakes!"

"A pup's dream," Oriole said, but his voice wasn't ridiculing. "You will always make mistakes, Delta. You must rise above them. Rise above your past mistakes."

"I will." I wavered for a second, so badly wanting to tell him about my dreams. But they were the dreams of a pup, right? They couldn't be real. "Thank you, Leader."

"You will do great things, young Delta," he nodded at me, then padded away.

I dipped my head. "I have great mentors."

"No, no, *no,* Delta!" Cynthia howled as I picked myself off the ground. "You should dive *beneath* the attack! You fell because you didn't!"

I groaned, then faced Peak once more. Poppy watched from the sidelines. I would think that watching me get beat to the ground would cheer her up, but no. My sister was just as melancholy as usual. I guessed it was because her training wasn't going well.

"You're nine moons old," Cynthia continued her bossy speech, "you should be able to fight!"

"Well, Peak's a little bigger than me, isn't he?" I shot back. He gave me an apologetic look.

Cynthia puffed out her furry chest. "I'm the same size as you and I can beat him up!"

"Hey!" Peak said good-naturedly.

"Well, that's because you're actually *good* at this." I plopped to the ground. "This is worse than memorizing spells and history."

"I'd rather learn this than what I've been learning," Poppy said glumly.

"I wonder when Oriole's going to choose a future leader." Peak changed the subject. "I mean, he *is* getting a *little* old."

"Don't say that!" I glared at him. "Oriole's a great leader!"

"But we *do* need a future leader," Cynthia said reasonably. "I mean, there's got to be *some* wolf he can choose."

"There has to be a prophecy about them," Poppy spoke up, "or he might choose the wrong wolf."

"Let's talk about something else," I snapped, glancing around the Crystal Cavern for things to talk about. "Like…" I spotted some Guardians entering the secret tunnel behind the waterfall. "Hey! What are *they* doing?"

"Going to the forest to find food," Peak said matter-of-factly. "Where do you think we get most of it?" He swelled up proudly. "My parents go on hunting missions. They're the best hunters in the Guardians!"

"That's cool," Cynthia said absentmindedly, staring after the wolves. She glanced back at us hopefully. "Do you think they'll allow a pup to accompany them?"

"Absolutely not," Mistflower snapped, padding up. "You are way too young, Cynthia."

"Mother!" I bounced around her. "Can you take us to the top of High Mountain? I want to go back up!"

I thought for a moment. "This time with adult supervision."

"Yeah!" Cynthia squealed.

Mistflower shook her head. "No! Not after what happened last time, and the time before that! Every time you pups go up there, you almost die!"

I groaned. "But I want excitement."

"Excitement means danger, and danger means imminent death." My mother was unmoving. "And on that note we will head to the Sleeping Chamber. It's late, and you four need sleep."

I exchanged an annoyed glance with Cynthia, Poppy, and Peak as we were herded into the Sleeping Chamber.

"Training to be a Power-Holder is awesome!" Lemon exclaimed after one particularly difficult lesson. "I mean, it's hard, but it all makes sense as you learn more!"

"Yeah," I agreed, as we padded down the dark tunnel. "I just wish Poppy was having more fun."

"She would if she could train with us," Boulder, the white pup, trotted up behind us. "I don't get why the Power-Holders have to give her private lessons, even if she *is* special."

My poor sister. While Cynthia and I had been excited at whatever we learned, Poppy had just grown more and more anxious. Couldn't Oriole and the other nine Power-Holders see that?

We padded into the Crystal Cavern together. I had half a mind to march up to Oriole and order him to leave my sister alone, natural power or not! But, of course, I was just a pup. That wasn't my place.

Just then a Guardian burst from the secret tunnel behind the waterfall. "Coyotes! They attacked me, Blade, and Luna while we hunted in the forest! I was running, and they were right behind me!"

Every wolf looked to the waterfall. The two wolves did not appear.

"We have to help them!" Peak howled, pounding toward the secret tunnel. Cynthia and I held him back.

Oriole's voice was grave. "Birch, go with Root and Ripple. Find Blade and Luna."

Birch, who was a respected warrior (as well as my father), nodded, and then rushed after the two Power-Holders.

I felt sick in my stomach. I hoped he would be all right.

Peak was still straining to follow them. "Let me go with them, Oriole!"

"Absolutely not," Oriole's voice was firm, "you are just a pup, Peak."

Peak then glared at the Guardian leader with so much ferocity and anger that I was surprised. I had never seen him like this.

But, of course, Blade and Luna were his parents.

Birch, Root, and Ripple returned soon, carrying the limp forms of Blade and Luna.

Peak stared at them. "Are they…?"

"No," Birch replied heavily. "We managed to kill the coyotes in time. But they are hurt."

Indeed, I could see blood oozing from numerous wounds on their bodies.

"Take them to the Healing Cave," Oriole said, "we will see which wounds are healable, and which ones need to be protected until they are healed."

The Guardians parted as the two injured wolves were carried to a tunnel and out of sight, Peak trailing after them.

A week later, Blade and Luna had nearly recovered from their wounds. But something was wrong. They were seriously sick. More wolves had gotten the disease. One had already died. The coyotes must have had a sickness in them, one that caused terrible sores, and now it had spread to the Guardians.

I was terrified about getting sick, but I couldn't stay away from the Healing Cave. My father, Birch, was sick. Mistflower, Cynthia, Poppy, and I stayed by his side every second. My chest was constricted with fear for him.

For every wolf.

Whatever this sickness was, it caused wolves to come down with a terrible fever, and to cough so much till blood came up. Then the unlucky wolf's hair would come out in some places, leaving ugly red sores.

Peak's parents, Blade and Luna, were worse than Birch, though. Peak stayed by their side, whimpering. He'd met my eyes once, his own filled with fear. I had sent what I hoped was a comforting look. But what comfort could I truly give?

Oriole and the Power-Holders had no idea what to do about the disease. That's what scared me.

I couldn't forget the moment Oriole had tried to heal Blade and Luna. Nothing had happened. The anger in Peak's eyes added to my worries.

More wolves died over the next few days. I feared that Birch would be among them, but he began to recover.

Blade and Luna didn't, though.

I knew the moment Peak's howls of anguish filled the Healing Cave.

"No!" He cried, frantically shaking Luna's body. "Mother!" He turned to Blade. "Father!" When they didn't answer, he collapsed, moaning.

"Peak…" I whispered, but he was oblivious to his surroundings. My head drooped and I slowly backed away. What could I possibly say?

Hopelessness hung in the air so thick I could scent it. The shadows around us seemed to be growing.

I felt sick with horror. What was next? *Who* was next?

The worst thing was that all the bad things that had been happening seemed connected to my dreams.

14

Birch had completely recovered. The sickness had not died out, though. Many Guardians had followed Blade and Luna to their graves.

I'd helped bury all the dead wolves in the forest below High Mountain. It was terrible, covering with earth the ones that had once walked, and laughed, and interacted with the world, now hollow shells of a past life.

I could never think about *that* too long.

Ever since the death of Peak's parents, he'd kept himself secluded from the rest of the Guardians. I didn't know what to say to him—what *could* I say? I'd never lost my parents before.

It bothered me how much anger he showed. I'd seen the fury in his eyes whenever he looked at Oriole or any of the other Power-Holders.

It was like he blamed them.

I found Peak staring into the water in the Crystal Cavern. "Hi."

He glanced at me, murky green eyes dim with pain. "Delta. Shouldn't you be in Power-Holder training?"

"I finished the lesson long ago," I sat next to his side. "Peak, it's already nighttime. Have you even eaten anything today?"

He shrugged. "Maybe. I don't remember." He continued to stare deeply into the water. "My mother used to tell me that whenever I looked up at the stars, I was seeing wolves of the past, spirits of nature. She said that one day she and Father would join the star wolves in their starry world, and that I would have to continue without them. I always told her that she and Father were so silly to suggest that they would someday die."

I nudged his shoulder. "Peak…"

"Don't tell me that it will all be okay in the end," he turned to me fiercely, "because it won't! I will never get over losing my parents! Never!"

"I'm not going to tell you that," I replied quietly, "I was going to say that you are not alone, Peak. I am your friend. If you ever need a wolf to talk to, I will be there. That's what friends are for."

He stared at me for a second, a strange expression on his face. Then he nodded slowly, turning back to the water.

We sat there for a long while. I hoped that I could help him overcome his sorrow, eventually.

Until then, I was as I had said.

His friend.

"No one gets me," Poppy stared straight ahead, not even touching the meat at her paws. "I don't want to be a Power-Holder."

"But it's your destiny," Birch said.

"And every wolf is very proud of you," Mistflower added.

Cynthia said something, but it was completely incomprehensible seeing that she had a chunk of meat hanging from her jaws.

I didn't know what to think. Poppy shouldn't be forced to be something she didn't want to be. But, on the other hand, she *did* have powerful Lostina that she obviously didn't have to replenish. My guess was because she had been born with it.

My family continued to talk, but I padded abruptly away, feeling their gazes on me.

Poppy was being forced into a role she didn't want to be in. She couldn't handle it. She was falling apart. I hated seeing her like this.

I didn't know what to do.

My life flew by faster than I could have ever thought. It seemed like only yesterday when I left the small cave to meet the Guardians for the first time. So much had happened since then.

No more wolves had died from the sickness, but its effect continued to add difficulties to life.

Peak had drawn away from any socialization. Poppy was doing the same—it scared me, how despairing she was becoming about her training. Cynthia was always talking about fighting. I continued studying.

And still, life flew by. I looked quite different from the puffy gray ball of fur I was when I had first entered the world. Mistflower said she was proud to have such lovely wolves as daughters, but I'm sure she just meant what was inside each of us.

Our insides were lovely, I guess.

I scoffed a little at that.

Poppy was a fine-enough pumpkin color, but I wouldn't call it pretty. Cynthia's creamy fur was always messy from her most recent scuffle. And of course, my fur was thick and stone-gray. A boring combination if you ask me.

I was learning some interesting things in Power-Holder training. I couldn't wait to be a Power-Holder! I imagined myself turning into a hawk, soaring on the winds of the world, fur *–feathers*— ruffling in the harsh breeze, far from any troubles—

"Delta!"

My eyes popped open. Lemon was padding up. "What are you thinking about? It looked like it was nice."

"Um…" I hesitated to tell her my silly thoughts. But, she *was* my friend and fellow Power-Holder in training. "Just how amazing it would be to fly."

"Yes!" Lemon said excitedly. "I can't wait to have powers! I want to become a fish!" She turned up her nose indignantly when I snorted, amused. "Being a fish would be amazing! I could swim!"

"Until a bigger fish comes along…" I trailed off, letting her think about it.

"Are you suggesting that I would get eaten?" She pretended to be angry.

I just shrugged.

"Well, I would be the biggest fish around," Lemon continued, "a huge fish, with long sharp *teeth!*" She snapped her jaws together.

"Uh, yeah…" I said doubtfully. "I'm pretty sure a fish like that does not exist."

She ignored me. "Anyways, have you *seen* Peak lately? He's always like this!" She made herself look so mournful I would have giggled if it wasn't for the fact that it was not funny.

"I feel so badly for him," I said softly.

Lemon nodded. "You know, he seems happy enough around you…"

"Shut up!" I snapped. "If Poppy hears you say that, she'll try to kill me in my sleep."

"That really does *not* sound like something she'd do," Lemon said cheerfully. "I bet that if you and Peak announced your mutual *love* in front of all the

Guardians, she wouldn't do anything about it. She's that nice."

"Yeah, you can stop talking now, Lemon," I muttered. This conversation was taking a direction I did *not* want to go. "I don't like Peak. It's as simple as that."

"Yeah, but he obviously likes you," Lemon replied evenly.

I glared at her. "This is such a ridiculous conversation. We should be drilling each other on what we learned in the lesson today."

"Delta, Delta, Delta," Lemon groaned playfully, "always the one to suggest we work and study."

"It's helpful!" I insisted. "We memorize things that way!"

Fortunately for Lemon, Cynthia pounded over. "Who wants to face me in a match?"

"Me!" Lemon said, and they headed over to a clear area in the Crystal Cavern, where I watched my sister promptly beat the older pup.

"And then the wolf reached the moon," Fern, the elder wolf, ended, "touching the skies."

"I've heard this story a *million* times," Cynthia groaned under her breath.

All the younger pups were listening to the story, but most of the older ones, having heard this tale all their life, had left.

I for one was always enthralled by the legend of the wolf that touched the stars. I still was, though I no longer believed it to be true.

Poppy had always enjoyed it as well. She sat beside me and Cynthia now, leaning forward with eager attention.

"Now it's time for those of you with training to go to your lessons," Fern rasped. When we all groaned, she clucked her tongue. "You should be eager to learn. You learn from learning."

I had stopped trying to understand everything the old wolf said long ago.

It wasn't that I didn't want to learn, though— of course I did! We were just learning the same things, over and over and over.

"Fur to feathers, scales to skin!" Lemon practiced as we padded to the new Training Cave. "Change me on the outside, but not from within!"

"That's great!" Boulder said, and I giggled at the look of absolute adoration in his eyes. "You're so awesome, Lemon!"

My friend hadn't noticed him trying to impress her for a while. I thought it was more than slightly hilarious.

My mind turned to Peak. Where *was* he nowadays? He never wanted to be with any of the other wolves. I felt so frustrated! He said he was happy to have me as a friend, but that didn't mean anything if he didn't let me help. He couldn't just lock himself away—he wasn't the only wolf to ever suffer!

As we all sat down, I tried to clear my mind. I learned more when I was focused.

"We'll be working on your fighting skills today." Stone glanced pointedly at me. "Some of you need… a little more practice."

I ducked my head, knowing he meant me. At least Cynthia wasn't here to embarrass me with her awesome fighting skills.

"We have a helper today," Stone nodded as a pup entered the Training Cave. "Cynthia."

My jaw dropped. A Power-Holder had asked my sister to help teach this lesson? The lesson *I* was participating in?

This was going to be so humiliating.

"Okay, pups," Cynthia said. Had she just called us *pups?!* "I'm here to show you how to fight! Who's first?" Her eyes lit up as she saw me. "Delta, how about you!"

My pelt flushed. This was going to be bad.

While Stone supervised, Cynthia and I stood across from each other.

"Ready?" she asked.

My eyes narrowed. I was not going to let her get away with showing off. "Only if you are."

Cynthia lunged at me, but I batted her away. I stared at my paws in surprise. I'd never done that move so well before.

She swung a paw at me, but I dodged, rolling out of the way.

This time I was on the offensive. I swung my forepaws at my sister, and she flung herself out of the way.

I was surprised I was still in the fight. This was the best I had ever done!

Then I let out a grunt as Cynthia knocked me to the ground. She stayed on top of me until I admitted defeat.

"I hope you all observed what moves were used in that fight," Cynthia shook her cream-colored fur, which was barely ruffled. "Now, split into teams of two. I will supervise. Alongside Stone, of course." She added quickly, glancing at the Power-Holder.

I knew my gray fur was sticking up everywhere. I hurriedly smoothed it before practicing with Lemon.

"Sorry if I embarrassed you, Delta," Cynthia whispered to me that night, curled in her bracken bed.

"It's fine," I whispered back, and I meant it—Cynthia was good at fighting. She really had taught us a lot.

I was just drifting to sleep when my ears picked up a slight noise. I cracked an eye open.

A small shape had just entered the Sleeping Chamber. Peak. Where had *he* been this late?

"Peak," I hissed at him. "What are you doing?"

He froze, turning to me. His eyes flashed in the darkness. "Just getting some water from the pond," he whispered back.

He then moved on to his bracken bed.

My brain swirled with questions. Peak had just lied to me. I could tell by his voice. And he had done it so *easily*.

Just like with Oriole.

I shook off my uneasiness. I was too cynical. Peak was my friend.

Sleep still fled from me.

15

"Twelve moons old! Twelve moons old! I am now twelve moons old!" Cynthia sang as she hopped out of her soft foliage bed.

The Guardians regarded the three of us with amusement as we all ran about. Even Poppy was excited.

And why shouldn't she be? I bounced cheerfully over to where Birch and Mistflower shared breakfast. "Father! Mother! We're a full year old!"

"And you've grown so much," Birch said proudly, "we couldn't have asked for better daughters, and High Mountain couldn't have better Guardians protecting it, and the Guardian Stone."

My tail wagged uncontrollably. "Just one more year and we'll be adults!"

"Yeah!" Poppy playfully nudged my shoulder.

The rest of the day was absolutely perfect. I managed to cheer up Peak (slightly), I got all the answers right in our lesson, and I played with my sisters and friends.

"This meat is *so* good!" Lemon sighed as we ate. "Even with it being winter and all."

"Yeah," I agreed. I noticed Peak enter the Crystal Cavern. "I'll be right back."

I hurried over to him. "Do you want to eat with us, Peak?"

His pale green eyes were as sad as ever, but I noticed something. Something like anger. "I'm not hungry," he said quietly.

"Then at least come sit with us," I pleaded, "please, Peak. We're your friends. We'll always be here for you."

"Yes," Poppy padded to my side, "always."

Peak's eyes filled with gratitude. "I guess I could eat a little bit."

"Then come on over here before all the meat's gone!" Cynthia hollered from across the Cavern.

Peak chuckled, and Poppy and I joined in. "Let's go, then." He began to head over there.

I nudged Poppy's shoulder. "Same thing goes for you, Poppy. You're my sister. Cynthia and I will always be here for you."

She returned the nudge. "Thanks, Delta."

The Guardians settled into the Sleeping Chamber later that night, and High Mountain was quiet. I stayed awake, waiting to see if Peak would go anywhere.

Finally, he silently rose from his bed and left.

I began to rise, but then Poppy mumbled sleepily, "where are you going, Delta?"

I froze, then plopped back into my bed. "Nowhere."

I tried to stay awake to see when Peak would return, but sleep overcame me.

I was in that horrible burning forest again.

"Stop it!" I howled as the three wolves sacrificed themselves to the darkness. "I've seen this before! Stop!"

Then I was floating in a dark void.

It was empty, yet… I could feel a presence. I didn't like it. Darkness was creeping in from all sides, blinding my eyes, suffocating me.

The next day wasn't as peaceful as the last. My dream— nightmare— haunted me. I knew that I had to tell Oriole.

But as I made my way to his chamber I paused. Those dreams couldn't be visions. I'd been having them since I was six moons old, and nothing had happened. I couldn't bother the Guardian leader with a pup's nightmares.

There was also a sick feeling deep in the pit of my stomach. I didn't want to know what that darkness was coming from. I wasn't brave enough to learn.

So I rerouted my paw steps to head to the Training Cave early, so I could study.

I stared at the tiny crystals emitting light that shone through the stone walls. This Training Cave was much cooler than the last one.

"Broken skin, come together…" I mumbled under my breath. "Lostina manifests its true power in those chosen…" I continued to go through my drills until Breeze led the Power-Holders-in-training into the cave.

"Delta! What are you doing here already?" she asked, surprised.

"Studying," I replied, trying not to sound too exhausted.

The Power-Holder nodded, pleased. "That is excellent, young one. This is what will turn one into a natural leader."

I wondered about her choice of words all through the lesson. It was about the Guardians' history, which I had already memorized. A wolf had discovered the Guardian Stone and created the Guardians. That was about it.

Afterwards, I padded down the passageway to where Poppy had her lessons. As I got closer, I heard a crashing sound—something I'd never heard from there before.

"Poppy?" I hurried into the cave. My eyes widened.

My sister was surrounded by some type of energy. It was expanding, and had knocked out a pillar. If it took any more out, the cave would collapse!

"Delta!" Root hurried up to me. "You must try and break through to her! She doesn't seem to hear me, but she might listen to you! She can't control it if she doesn't calm down!"

Heart racing, I nodded. I faced Poppy once more. She looked terrified.

"Poppy!" I shouted, but she couldn't seem to hear me. I moved toward the energy surrounding her.

"No, Delta!" Root said. "You will be torn apart!"

"She's my sister!" I shouted. "I have to reach her!"

At that moment she noticed me. *Delta?*

I started as her voice rang out in my head. "Don't worry, it's okay! Just take a few deep breaths. Imagine you are pulling the power back within you."

My copper-colored sister nodded, still looking scared. She closed her eyes.

I heaved out a sigh of relief as the energy drew back into her. She took a few trembling steps, then collapsed.

"Poppy!" I rushed to her side. "Root! What do we do?!"

The older wolf shook his head. "I don't know. I believe she is just exhausted."

"What happened?" I flinched at the accusing sound of my voice. I shouldn't talk to a Power-Holder like that!

Root overlooked my rudeness. "I was teaching your sister how to shapeshift. She lost control of her power. We used to think her special Lostina was a gift, but now…" He looked around the unstable chamber. "I am not so sure about that."

16

"I'm a monster!" Poppy whimpered when she woke up in the empty Sleeping Chamber.

"No, you aren't!" I said fiercely, and Cynthia nodded vigorously.

"But I lost control," Poppy's eyes were scared. "I could have destroyed High Mountain!"

"But you didn't!" Cynthia's voice was cheerful. "Everything turned out okay!"

I flinched. That was *not* what Poppy needed to hear right now.

She hung her head. "I wish I'd never had this power. I hate it."

Birch and Mistflower entered the Sleeping Chamber. "Are you okay, Poppy?" our mother asked worriedly.

My sister didn't reply, just turned away from us. I struggled to hold in my frustration.

"We are the only Guardians that know," Birch said soothingly. Our father laid a paw on Poppy's shoulder. "Besides Oriole and the other Power-Holders, of course."

"The Guardians don't need me," Poppy said softly, turning back to us. The look in her eyes gave me a feeling of foreboding.

"That's a lie!" Cynthia glared at her. "We *do* need you in the Guardians, Poppy! And it's not because of your power! It's because you're you, and you're my sister!"

"Yeah!" I agreed fervently.

"I want to be alone," Poppy said quietly. I recognized the look in her eyes. My stomach dropped.

We reluctantly left her to rest. I was sure I had had the same look in my eyes when I'd been about to run away. But that had been different. I had been running from facing the consequences for my mistake. Poppy obviously didn't like her role. What if she was *meant* to leave?

The thought horrified me, but I remembered when all the pups had learned of callings. Every wolf had one eventually. What if Poppy's calling was not here, with us?

But that's impossible, I thought, desperately trying to erase what I was thinking. *Poppy's meant to be here with us. We're her family.*

I pulled behind Birch, Mistflower, and Cynthia. Making sure they didn't notice me, I crept back into the Sleeping Chamber.

Poppy glanced up at me. "Delta. What are you doing here? I thought I said I wanted to be alone."

"I know," I forced myself to go on, "but I have to tell you something."

My copper-furred sister sighed. "Okay. Go ahead."

"Remember when I ran away?" I asked. When she nodded, I went on. "I told Sky that if she went to the Boglands and back, that she would instantly become a Power-Holder. I didn't think that she'd actually listen to me. She… well, you know what happened."

Poppy cocked her head. "What does this have to do with me?"

"I ran away because of the guilt I felt," I said, "I shouldn't have. If it wasn't for Peak, I would still be out there." I thought for a second. "Actually, I'd probably be dead. Anyways, my point is, I ran away from facing the guilt."

Poppy glanced down at her paws. "I'm not trying to run away from anything."

"I know," I said evenly, though it was a struggle to keep my voice from breaking, "and I have to ask you this— do you feel that your calling is with the Guardians?"

My sister took in a deep breath. There was silence for a moment. Then she met my eyes. "No. I don't."

I felt like whimpering, but that would be too immature. I wanted Poppy to live away from stress. She deserved more than that. "I guess you'll find a place to call home."

Poppy nodded. "Yeah, I guess. You'll help me, right?"

"Of course," I promised, "and I— I hope we meet again, Sister."

"Sister." Poppy nuzzled my shoulder. She stood. "I am ready."

My belly constricted, but I nodded. "I will always be here for you."

She seemed to waver for a second, then padded briskly into the tunnel that led to the Crystal Cavern.

Oriole and the Power-Holders were chatting at the base of the Guardian Stone. Cynthia was sharing a meal with our parents.

"I hope I'm not walking away from my destiny," Poppy stared at the Guardian Stone.

"You'll discover new lands," I crept to her side, "you will maybe even find a pack."

She whirled to face me, eyes watery. "Tell Cynthia and our parents that I love them. I love you, Delta."

"I love you, my sister," I said solemnly.

She wagged her tail slightly, then crept around the Crystal Cavern, to the waterfall. Before she left, she glanced at me.

I saw a flash of her brown eyes before they vanished.

My tail drooped between my legs, and my ears flattened. Poppy was gone. My sister was gone.

"Poppy's gone." I trudged up to my parents and remaining sister.

"What?" Mistflower shot to her paws. "What do you mean, *gone?"*

"She's not in the Sleeping Chamber," I replied.

"Oriole!" Birch howled.

The Guardian leader rose to his paws. The Guardians began to gather around. "What is it, Birch?"

"Poppy's gone!" Mistflower cried.

Oriole's eyes widened, and he crossed an arch to stand with us. "Search all around. She could be in another chamber."

I searched with the others, knowing that we weren't going to find anything. Mistflower let out a screeching cry. "She must have run away!"

"She was under a lot of stress," Birch said worriedly.

"HOW?!" Cynthia howled. "How could she do this?!"

A wolf crept to my side. It was Peak. His eyes met mine, and I saw the sorrow in his eyes, mingled with a question.

I nodded.

With a whimper, he turned and padded away.

17

The Guardians were in an uproar about Poppy. Every wolf had expected her to lead the Guardians someday. I mostly just sat around numbly, Cynthia by my side. I had never lost anyone before so close to me before, even if Poppy *wasn't* dead.

"How will she defend herself?" Cynthia moaned.

I shrugged. "She'll find a way." But doubt invaded my thoughts. Poppy was so sweet and timid. What if she ran into coyotes, or hostile wolves? Or cougars?

I abruptly stood and padded to a more secluded area of the Crystal Cavern, where I was left to my own thoughts.

For seconds.

"Delta." Peak came up, looking just as sad as he always did. "You let Poppy leave."

"Yes," I said quietly, "I did."

He stared at his paws for a moment. "I'm upset that she felt she had to leave. I hope she finds whatever it is she's looking for."

"Home," I said, "she's looking for a home."

A look of such deep longing came over his face, I had to look away.

"Home." He repeated softly.

"Those with special talents often have great burdens," Oriole addressed the Guardians. "Such is what happened with Poppy. We can only hope she's heading for a greater calling."

"But what can be greater than being a future Power-Holder?" The elder wolf, Fern, croaked.

"Sometimes great things don't come from power," the Guardian leader replied. "Poppy wanted something more than that."

I suddenly found myself marching to the front of all the Guardians. "She did."

Every wolf turned to me. Oriole dipped his head, allowing me to go on.

"Poppy did have an amazing gift," I said. My voice sounded small in the echoing Crystal Cavern. "And that's how many saw her. As a future Power-Holder. Possibly even leader. But to me, and Cynthia, she was a sister. She had a kind heart, and she always brought light to our days. That's what I remember, and that's what mattered. I don't care about her powerful magic— she had a heart that could light the dark. She didn't need powerful Lostina."

Silence stretched on. My paws twitched uncomfortably. *I really should know my place!*

Then Birch and Mistflower began howling, low and meaningfully. Cynthia joined in, then Lemon, Boulder, and the other Power-Holders in training. Even Sky started howling. Peak met my eyes, then began howling as well.

Poppy would be missed. I wondered if she could hear us now. Oriole's eyes held pride. Cynthia crept to my side and nuzzled my shoulder.

As long as the rest of us kept together, we would all be okay.

I set to my studies vigorously. Just because one of my sisters was gone didn't give me an excuse to shirk my duties. Besides, it helped take my mind off Poppy's absence, Peak's aloofness and my dreams.

Days passed by. Poppy didn't return. Wolves stopped reassuring us that she would run right back to the Guardians with her tail between her legs. It was obvious that she wasn't coming back.

I sighed, listening as Wisp explained the difference between Lostina and Vestina. *Again.*

Finally, the lecture was over. I hurried out of the Training Cave, Lemon and Boulder at my heels.

To my surprise, the Guardian leader was waiting there.

"Leader," I said quickly, bowing my head. My two friends copied me.

"Young Delta," Oriole rumbled, "will you follow me?" Then he turned and headed down a branch-off tunnel.

I exchanged a confused glance with Lemon and Boulder, then, after saying goodbye, hurried after the older wolf.

He led me into the cave where Poppy had once trained. "Ever since you were born, the Power-Holders— including myself— noticed that you have a natural skill."

I cocked my head to the side. "Really?"

"Yes," he said briskly, "you are loyal, Delta. You give orders strictly, but not harshly. You are the top of everything you do— besides fighting, of course. You are a natural leader."

"Leader?" My gut clenched. Of course. Oriole wanted me to be the next leader.

"The Guardian Stone showed it to me," the Guardian leader continued, "in a vision, before you were born. You will lead when I am gone, Delta."

My head began to spin. This was all so much to take in. "I don't think I can do it!"

"You can," his voice held not a hint of doubt. "I know that."

"When do I begin training?" My voice came out as barely a whisper.

"Tomorrow," Oriole replied. "Sunshine will lead you to where you should go. You already know many things, but there is more."

It felt like the ground was falling away beneath my paws. My vision blurred. This was what I'd always wanted.

To be great.

I entered the Crystal Cavern, heart pounding. My entire future had just been changed in the space of a few minutes.

Leader. That couldn't be right. *I* couldn't be the right wolf.

But I knew I was.

The Guardian leader padded up to the Guardian Stone, then turned to face all the wolves. "Guardians! I have an announcement to make!"

"I wonder what it could be," Mistflower said as she, Birch, and Cynthia came to sit with me. I shrugged, but my insides roiled.

"We have a leader in training!" Oriole howled. The Guardians immediately erupted into cheers, but he silenced them with a flick of his tail. "She is a very talented pup. I had a vision that she was the one."

"Who is it already?" Peak called from nearby.

"Delta!" Howls of excitement filled the Cavern.

I shrank back as all eyes turned to me. My parents and sister's jaws all hung open. Lemon and Boulder's eyes were as wide as the moon. Peak was staring in shock.

"Thank you," was all I could manage before the din continued.

That's when I realized that with Poppy gone and me moving to a leader in training, there were two empty Power-Holder in training spots.

"I have suggestions for who to make the two new Power-Holders in training!" I called out excitedly as the idea struck me.

All became silent. I flinched. *Delta, you're being too bold again!* "I mean, if you are fine with it, Leader…"

"Of course," Oriole dipped his head at me, "go on, young Delta."

"Sunflower," I said quickly. The brown-and-white she-pup looked stunned, but she stood as the Guardians cheered.

"Young Sunflower," Oriole told her, "you deserve this title, I am sure. You will make a good Power-Holder!"

She nodded vigorously. "Thank you thank you thank you!"

Oriole met my eyes. "Who is your second choice?"

I hesitated for a moment, then turned to look at the young black she-wolf that sat nearby. "Sky."

Murmurs went through the crowd. Sky shot up and faced me, though her blind eyes stared in another direction. "Why me? In case none of you have noticed, I'm *blind!*"

"But you persevere," Oriole replied. "You don't give up. You're brave. Just because you can't see doesn't mean that you cannot feel. You will make a good Power-Holder."

Howls erupted, calling her name. Sky's jaw dropped, but her tail began to wag, slower at first, then faster.

Cynthia rammed into me playfully. "My sister, future leader!"

I chuckled, then began to laugh fully. This was what I was made for— leading.

And I was ready to begin.

"Peak," I said, padding up to him. It had taken a while, but I'd finally broken away from the mob of Guardians wanting to congratulate me.

His head snapped toward me, then he stared at his paws. "I'm happy for you, Delta."

His voice didn't fit what he'd just said. My stomach felt like it was dropping in slow motion. Wasn't he glad?"

"I should go," he said, and with that, he left.

I stared after him, feeling empty. We were friends. Why was he acting like this? Then I set my jaw. I was going to find out what was up with him.

I followed Peak late that night, as he crept out of the Sleeping Chamber. I was going to find out what he was doing!

He silently slipped past the guards in the Crystal Cavern, vanishing up the tunnel that led to the summit of High Mountain. I followed.

I crept to his side as he stood on the edge of the mountain, paws crunching in the snow. The gusts of wind blew swirls of the white powder across the ground.

"I figured you'd follow me out here eventually," Peak spoke first.

"Why are you coming out here?" I asked.

He sighed. "To think. And concentrate. I've been… well, I've been getting better every day."

"At what?" I turned my head to look at him. "Concentrating?"

He didn't answer, just looked upwards. I followed his gaze.

The night sky was clear, the moon shining like a bright silver pool of light in an endless abyss of shadow. Thousands of stars clumped together, forming shapes, some even swirling with color. "It's beautiful."

"Yeah," Peak said quietly, "I imagine Mother and Father up there." He met my eyes. "Do you think they're watching me?"

"I know they are," I replied.

He held my gaze for a moment, then looked back into the sky.

I stood there with him for the rest of the night, watching as stars began to shoot across the sky, almost as if they were falling.

18

My paws tingled with anxiety as I pattered after Sunshine, one of the Power-Holders. We padded through a stone tunnel, going deeper and deeper into the mountain.

My tail twitched, and I shivered at the chilly air.

"Our leader is anxious to begin your training," Sunshine broke the uneasy silence. "He is growing old."

"I'm a little nervous," I admitted.

The blonde-furred wolf gave me an encouraging nudge. "Of course you are, Delta. You're about to be in training to be a leader."

We lapsed back into silence. I struggled to see as my paws slipped and slid on the grimy stone. I flinched every time a freezing drop of water pierced into my fur and skin.

After what seemed ages, we emerged into a small round room, with a domed ceiling made entirely of crystal. Light streamed through the precious stone, lighting up a similar crystal platform that sat right beneath.

My jaw dropped. It was beautiful. "What is this place?" I asked, then realized Sunshine was gone. Her scent drifted back the way we had come.

"Welcome, young Delta."

I nearly fainted from surprise and shock as the dark red wolf with green eyes emerged from the shadows.

"This is the Crystal Dais." Oriole's eyes were sympathetic as I stared at him, trembling. "Only me and the other nine Power-Holders know that it exists, and I'd like it to stay that way. It is a bridge between reality and the Unending Cycle. It allows me to visit the Crystal Forest."

I let out a stammering noise, then cleared my throat, trying to look dignified in front of my leader. "That's neat." I winced. That was not the right word to describe this.

Oriole chuckled softly. I noticed that his muzzle was graying, and there were gray flecks in his fur. He moved with difficulty. He seemed older than most elder wolves, now that I actually noticed!

He chuckled again at my shyness. "I am old, I know. You have much to learn, Delta."

"Great!" I bounced on my paws. "What's first?" My eyes widened. "Am I going to the Crystal Forest?"

Oriole actually laughed this time. "Not today, young one. Today you will see what you must protect as leader of the Guardians."

I tilted my head. "The Guardian Stone, right? The source of all light?"

"True," he rumbled, "but so much more than that. Look into the Crystal Dais."

I did as I was told, though it felt pretty silly to stare at a solid platform of crystal. Then its surface rippled, and I gasped as I found myself soaring on the strongest gust of wind I had ever felt.

I let out a cry of terror when I realized that I was high inside clouds.

Below was the world.

It was bigger than I ever could have imagined. There was High Mountain, looming high above earth, tall peaks rising to meet the sky. A massive forest stretched around the mountain, wide and green. And there, at the end of it, was a small swamp forest. It was bright and green, filled with life. In fact, the whole world pulsed with life.

There was more, but before I could get a close look at it, I was back in the cave. The Crystal Dais was as still as it had been before.

"Wow!" I shrieked, whirling to face Oriole. "That was *awesome!*"

"Yes, it was," the Guardian leader said, amused. "I felt just as excited when I began training." His eyes grew troubled. "Being leader is also about receiving messages from the Guardian Stone. It is about having dreams, or visions, often which are not pleasant."

I flinched, thinking about the dreams I'd been having. Maybe they really *were* visions.

"You look distressed, young Delta," Oriole said, a concerned edge to his voice.

"I…" *Should I tell him? What if he just says that I had a foolish nightmare, or am trying to get more attention? What if I'm better off not knowing what my dreams are about? What if he thinks I'm crazy?* I hated myself for not speaking up when I'd first had the vision many moons ago. "I just can't believe there's so much beyond High Mountain! I mean, I've known that, but never from the sky."

"There is far more than what you saw today," my leader replied.

"Great!" I said enthusiastically. "I want to see it *all!*"

The russet-furred wolf's tail gave a slight wag. "You should return to your friends now, Delta. We are finished here."

"What?" A prickle of irritation ran along my spine. "But we only just started. I want to learn more!"

Orioles' eyes were understanding but firm as he spoke. "Seeing our world was enough for today. It is filled with life, but darkness can creep in. We must protect the source of all light."

"The Guardian Stone," I said automatically.

As I left the small cave, I thought about my dreams. I really should tell some wolf…

I will when the time feels right. I thought uneasily.

But that was the problem, wasn't it? I didn't *want* to know. I was afraid of what would change when I did.

I had learned pretty much the same things since my first day with Oriole. Lostina… Guardian Stone… Nothing new. But I still paid attention to every detail.

I had finally used the Crystal Dais to see into the past. The Dais was so powerful because it channeled energy from the Guardian Stone.

As I padded down to the "Mystic Cave" as I called it, I skipped excitedly. Today I would be peering into the future! I probably wouldn't be able to see as far, like with the past, but it would still be cool.

I finally emerged into the Mystic Cave, where my mentor waited, sitting beside the Crystal Dais.

"Welcome, Delta," Oriole rumbled, "are you ready?"

I nodded. "Yes."

"Then we will begin." He peered into the Crystal Dais. "Look into the future, Delta. See things no other has seen before." His voice echoed strangely.

I crept up to the edge of the crystal platform, peering inside. I could see my reflection, distorted, deep within.

Images flashed before my eyes. A forest. Then a snowy plain. The snow was streaked with blood. There was the Mystic Cave, the crystals inside all smashed. Darkness. There was darkness.

With a yelp, I pulled back.

"What is it?" Oriole was at my side, alarmed. "What did you see, Delta?"

"Darkness," I choked out. My heart was pounding so hard I could barely breathe. "And blood. Lots of it."

Oriole glanced into the Crystal Dais for a moment, then looked back at me. "I did not see anything, but that does not mean that what you saw isn't real." He fully faced me. "I ask this as your mentor and leader—have you seen things like this before?"

"Yes," I whispered, staring at my paws, "ever since I was six moons old. I never wanted to seem like I was trying to get attention, though. I—I thought they were only nightmares."

Oriole sighed, closing his eyes. When he opened them, they were exasperated. "Delta, you don't ignore visions, especially ones like what you've been having. It seems that something terrible is coming."

"I don't know quite what, though," I said. Now that I was no longer keeping the visions to myself, I felt free.

But I really was the stupidest pup in all history for not telling him sooner.

"Try to look again," Oriole replied.

I nodded, then peered into the Crystal Dais. Red. Darkness. Three wolves.

With a screech of pain, I pulled away. "I can't do this anymore!" My eyes watered, and I blinked rapidly, clawing at my face as if that would take away the dark images.

"It's okay," my mentor said soothingly, but his eyes were grim, "you *can* do this. You have to."

I slowly raised my face up to him. "There's nothing but pain, blood, and darkness."

"You can rest now," Oriole nudged my ear reassuringly. "You have done your part."

19

I kept expecting something terrible to happen, but life went on. Peak continued to drift farther away—we'd barely spoken since that night on the top of the mountain. It grew harder and harder to speak to my family, as my leader training lasted all day every day.

Oriole told me to always be ready.

Ready for what?

I didn't want to find out.

The time finally came for me to enter the Crystal Forest. I padded into the Mystic Cave, excited but anxious about what I would find.

"Are you ready, Delta?" My mentor asked. When I nodded, he continued. "Good. Now, go and stand on the Crystal Dais."

I stepped up onto the platform, feeling quite silly. Then I was falling, and suddenly found myself… still standing on the Dais.

My surroundings were no longer stone.

I stood in a forest. But it wasn't just any forest. The foliage sparkled with a frost-like look. The grass crunched softly when I put a paw on it.

"Wow," I breathed, taking it all in. I stood in the Crystal Forest.

I eagerly began to pad through. It was beautiful here. Everything sparkled.

But as I kept walking, I realized that everything looked the same. My heart fluttered slightly. What if I needed the Crystal Dais to get back?

"Hello?" My voice echoed strangely. No voices answered. I was alone.

Whirling around, I started heading back the way I'd came, but the Dais was nowhere in sight.

"Oriole?" I called uncertainly. "Can you hear me? I want to go back to the Mystic Cave."

Immediately I stood on the Crystal Dais, in the Mystic Cave. With a sigh of relief, I stepped off the platform.

"What did you find, Delta?" Oriole asked. "Who spoke to you?"

"No wolf," I told my mentor, "I was alone."

"That's strange," he muttered, more to himself. Then he returned his gaze to me. "No glowing paw prints?"

"Uh," I said, trying to imagine *that,* "no."

Oriole looked concerned for a moment, but then began to leave the Mystic Cave. "You did well for your first time, Delta. We will try again tomorrow."

With a sigh, I followed him.

"Hey, Peak!" I called as I saw him in a secluded corner of the Crystal Cavern, eyes closed.

My friend opened his eyes, and they lit up when he saw me. "Delta! Have you told Oriole about your visions?"

"Of course," I replied. I felt a little guilty for not telling Peak what Copper had said about darkness and light, but I strangely felt like I should keep it to myself, even from him.

"I'm glad you're going to be leader someday," he said, breaking the silence. "I know you'll be great. I'm sorry for how I acted. I truly am happy for you. And it was nice of you to ask if Sunflower and Sky could be future Power-Holders."

"They deserve it," I said. I thought about how excited Sunflower had been, practically bouncing off the stone walls. And Sky was doing well. She still remembered a lot from old lessons, so she was able to keep up with the rest. I felt a happy tingling in my paws, knowing that he really *was* glad for me.

Thinking about Lemon didn't make me as happy, though. I still played with her, but now leader training was taking up a lot of my life, and she likewise had Power-Holder training.

Cynthia was still having fighting lessons, as was Peak, and they were both pretty good at it.

"Delta," Peak tilted his head, an amused glint in his eyes, "you're drifting off into your thoughts. *Again.*"

I rolled my eyes as he snorted in laughter. "Whatever. I have a lot to think about."

"It's been four moons since Poppy left," Peak's voice grew more melancholy, "do you ever miss her?"

"Of course I do," I replied right away, feeling the familiar pain in my heart as it throbbed, "she was my sister. I just hope she's found a home."

"Yeah," he said, shuffling his paws, "she used to like me, I think. When we were little pups."

"Yeah," I chuckled, remembering, "it was hilarious."

"Have you ever thought about the future, Delta?" Peak asked.

I nodded. "Of course. All the time."

"I mean," he glanced down at his paws awkwardly, "if you're ever going to fall in love with a wolf."

"Maybe," I said dubiously.

He looked at me hopefully. "That's great!"

I stared at him for a second, then realized what he was trying to say. "Oh, you mean *you?*" My voice came out sounding amused.

His eyes dropped back to the ground. "Never mind."

"No, no," I said quickly, "you're a good wolf, Peak. I'll consider you in the future."

"Really?" His tail wagged slightly. "That's awesome! Thanks, Delta!" He trotted off.

I watched him go, then realized my own tail was wagging. *That's weird.*

I padded in a different direction than he took, not noticing that there was a spring in *my* paw steps.

I stood on top of High Mountain. I could see the forest below me. It was on fire.

A wave of darkness swept across the land far below. When it subsided, the forest was gone, only dry, cracked plain.

"It is coming, Delta," Shade, the older wolf, came to stand beside me. Willow and Copper joined me as well.

"But not a little while more," Willow turned to gaze at me.

"When?" I asked. "When will I know?"

"When darkness overcomes what was once light," Copper replied.

I nodded slowly, feeling a rising sense of dread at those ominous words. My vision faded, and I was gone, into the darkness.

"It will come when darkness overcomes what was once light!" I told Oriole eagerly that morning.

The Guardian leader's eyes were thoughtful. "That could mean a number of things." Then he glanced up at the Guardian Stone, which rose above us.

"You don't think the Guardian Stone will die, do you?" I gasped in horror at the thought.

"I do not know," Oriole's voice was grave, "but we will be ready for whatever it is. Who were those three wolves in your vision?"

"Shade, Copper, and Willow," I replied. "I think they were Guardians once."

"I do not know the names," my mentor mused, "but they could have lived in the past."

"They saved the forest from the darkness once," I said. "Maybe they're trying to tell us exactly how to do that."

"Perhaps," Oriole replied. "Tell me if you have any more visions, Delta. And thank you."

"Yes, Oriole," I dipped my head to him, then padded away. It felt great to be spoken to like an adult wolf!

But the pleased feeling in my chest drained away as I realized the responsibility that was about to be thrust upon me would be the responsibility *of* an adult wolf.

20

I was padding through the Crystal Cavern when a terrible pain hit my head. With a cry, I collapsed to the ground.

"Delta!" Several wolves rushed to my side.

"Delta?" Cynthia peered down at me. I could barely see anything, though. My vision was growing darker.

Then a wolf pushed his way up to me. Oriole. "What is it, Delta? What's wrong?"

"Darkness," I whispered, surprising myself, "in High Mountain. In the Guardians." The pain suddenly stopped, and I sat up, wondering where what I had just said came from.

Oriole's face was grim. "Are you sure?"

"I…" I tried to sense the pain again, but it had vanished completely. "I don't know. I could feel it, though."

The Guardians all looked worried, whispering and peering around as if something was creeping up on them.

"I believe you," Oriole said firmly, "can you stand?"

"Yeah," I grunted, rising.

"Delta!" Peak rushed through the crowd of wolves. "I heard you cry out! Are you okay?"

I blinked at him, grateful that he was worried for me. "I'm fine."

"She thinks there's darkness in the Guardians!" Cynthia told him.

Peak's eyes widened, but he said nothing.

"Not just any darkness," I looked at Oriole urgently, "Vestina."

I was sure every wolf gasped and winced at the word. Oriole looked out over the Guardians. "Really? Vestina?"

"Yes," I was sure, "I felt it!"

"But if that's true, we have an evil wolf in our midst!" Sky howled, blind eyes agitated.

I was just as nervous. Vestina in the Guardians? I had to be wrong.

But I wasn't.

"Just so you know, Delta," Peak said unexpectedly, "no matter what happens, I like you, and I'll die if it means it will protect you."

I stared at him, embarrassed that he had just said that in front of all the Guardians. I noticed Lemon's smug look. "Er, thanks, Peak," I said awkwardly.

He nodded, looking kind of upset. Well, he had a reason to be, for just saying that in front of every wolf!

"Delta's fine!" Oriole called to all the Guardians. "She needs time. You may all return to whatever you were doing before."

They all drifted away, including Peak. Only my parents, Cynthia, and Lemon stayed.

"Tell me if you feel anything else, Delta," Oriole said seriously. "This is a very grave situation."

"Of course," I replied. Then I realized something. "This is the light consumed by darkness, isn't it?"

"It seems so," Oriole said, "just be careful, young one." He padded off to talk with the Power-Holders about what had just happened.

"I told you Peak liked you!" Lemon nudged me.

"And you like him!" Cynthia crowed.

I rolled my eyes. "Whatever."

"Delta, are you sure you're okay?" Birch asked worriedly.

"Yes, Father," I groaned, "I'm fine." Then I stiffened. Whoever had been infected with Vestina was using it. "But maybe not for long."

Not for long at all.

I kept feeling the darkness. It was always close by, but I couldn't place exactly where. Every day was an increasing sense of dread in the Guardians. I racked my brain every night, trying to think of possible wolves that could have the darkness. Then, one day (which would be one of the worst days of my life, though I didn't know it), I had an idea.

I stretched out in my bed in the Sleeping Chamber, listening to all the snores. It was horrible to think that one of them had Vestina. They would have to be angry, bitter, or anything like that to have it.

My eyes widened. A terrible lump formed in my throat. Without a sound, I rose to my paws. I crept over to where Peak usually slept. His bracken bed was empty.

…to think. And concentrate. I've been… well, I've been getting better every day.

"No," I whispered, desperately hoping I was wrong. I slipped out of the Sleeping Chamber, through the Crystal Cavern, and into the tunnel that led to the top of High Mountain.

I slowly popped my head out into the cold night air. My mouth went dry.

A dark gray wolf stood with his back to me, muttering strange words. Oily black energy flowed around him.

I knew I had to get Oriole, but… if I did, Peak would be banished. I had to convince him to stop!

"Peak." I stepped fully into the open.

He whirled around, and I gasped. His green eyes were filled with black, but they returned to normal when he saw me. "Delta?! What are you doing up here?"

"I had a hunch," I said coolly, "and I was right."

"No!" Peak's voice was desperate. "That wasn't what it looked like!"

"Stop talking, Peak!" I shouted at him so fiercely that he snapped his muzzle shut. "I know what that was! Vestina! You've been using darkness!" I glared at him, wanting to claw his face off. I'd been betrayed by the wolf that wanted to share the future with me, and I was *mad.*

"I lost my parents," Peak stared down at his paws, "then Poppy left. I don't know how it happened, but this power *found* me, Delta. It's really not that bad!"

"I can't believe this," I stared at him, seeing him as he really was for the first time, "I thought you liked me."

"I do!" He said profoundly. "I love you, Delta!"

"Then let it go." I met his imploring gaze unflinchingly. "Let the Vestina go, or you will have to leave the Guardians."

"I can't believe you'd want that, Delta," he said defensively.

"I don't!" My voice began to rise to a higher pitch. "But right now we're on separate sides, Peak! We're *enemies!"*

By now morning was beginning to dawn. I knew the Guardians were waking. "Give it *up!"*

"I can't," Peak began to back away, "it's power."

"Then I have no choice." I lunged at him, claws and teeth flashing. With a yelp, he ducked out of the way, but I managed to snag his fur.

He winced at the cut. "It doesn't have to be like this, Delta."

"Yes it does, Peak." I slashed at his face, but he pulled back.

"What's going on up here?" A voice shouted. I whirled around to see Oriole standing there. He took one glance at me, then at Peak and his bleeding flank.

My heart was breaking. I really *did* like Peak. I loved him. But I was the light. He was the dark. "Peak is using Vestina."

Oriole cast a withering gaze upon the young wolf. "Peak?"

Peak didn't respond, but he muttered something. A blast of dark power shot toward Oriole.

"Oriole!" I screeched, but my mentor was ready. He used his power to create a shield, then bounded at Peak and knocked him to the ground, where he lay unconscious.

I gulped down a sob. "I'm sorry I didn't realize it sooner. I should have known what he was doing."

"No," Oriole turned to me, "I am sorry, Delta. I know how you two felt about each other."

"Yeah," I said quietly, staring at the unmoving gray wolf, "but I had a choice to make. I chose the Guardians."

21

All the Guardians stood around Peak in the Crystal Cavern.

Oriole strode up to him. "Peak, your desire for power has consumed you."

"No!" Peak whimpered. "I'm not power-hungry! I just wanted to get rid of my pain! Tell them, Delta!" He turned to me.

I shook my head, struggling not to break down into sobs. Cynthia stood at my side, glaring at him.

"Vestina has a hold on your heart," the Guardian leader went on. "There's only one judgement for that."

"No…" Peak whined, crouching to the ground. "Please…"

"You are banished from the Guardians," Oriole said sternly. "Leave, and if you are ever seen around High Mountain again, you will pay with your life."

"Oriole, please—" I began, but my mentor silenced me with a flick of his tail.

"No, Delta. He is no longer a pup. He must feel the consequences of his actions."

I took a deep breath, then nodded, stepping back.

"Fine." Peak's voice was hard. "Turn your backs on me, all of you! I *will* have my revenge." He turned and stalked through the Guardians, vanishing down the secret tunnel. All was silent for a few minutes.

"Make sure he's left, Sunshine," Oriole told the Power-Holder. She nodded, then padded behind the waterfall and out of sight.

"Are you all right, Delta?" Mistflower nudged my shoulder softly.

"I will be," I said quietly. Then I turned and left the Crystal Cavern.

I awoke to a horrible shrieking noise. Leaping out of my bracken bed, I followed the stream of worried Guardians as they surged into the Crystal Cavern.

I took one look at the Guardian Stone, then gasped. It was surrounded by black power.

"Delta!" Oriole and the other Power-Holders bounded up. "It's come! Be prepared to do whatever is necessary!"

I nodded shakily. Lemon, Boulder, Ruby, Goldenrod, Reed, Dewdrop, and Elderberry pounded up, followed by Cynthia. Sky raced after them, moving surprisingly well despite her blindness.

"What do you need us to do, Delta?" she asked.

"Evacuate High Mountain," I replied, "we need to get the Guardians out of here."

They immediately set off. Cynthia stayed beside me, and we watched as Oriole and the others shot power at the Stone. "I don't think I can fight this with my claws, Delta," she said.

I faced her. "You won't have to. Oriole knows what he's doing."

At that moment I heard the Guardian leader's panicked voice. "Get out of here!"

Whirling, my jaw dropped open. Oriole and the Power-Holders were racing away from the Guardian Stone, which was now pitch-black. The dark power was spreading out from it, crossing the water…

By now most of the Guardians had fled through the secret tunnel. I nosed Cynthia after them before racing up to my fellow Power-Holders in training. "You all need to get out of here!"

"What about you?" Lemon asked.

Sky stamped a paw. "We're not leaving you, Delta. We fight together."

"We are *all* leaving!" Oriole was at our side. "Get to the tunnel, now!"

We raced after him, the only wolves left in the Crystal Cavern. As they all thundered down the secret tunnel, I hesitated, looking back.

By now my home was covered in darkness. Swallowing a sob, I bounded after the others.

We emerged into the forest, just as morning dawned. We stood with the Guardians and watched as darkness covered High Mountain.

"Whenever a Guardian allows darkness into their heart, it can corrupt the Guardian Stone," Oriole said. He turned to me. "How did the wolves in your vision defeat the darkness?"

I hesitated, but he needed to know. "They had to—"

"It's coming!" A wolf howled in terror. My eyes shot to the sky, and my heart dropped.

A giant wall of blackness rose above High Mountain, just as terrible as it had been in my vision.

But this time it was *really* here.

A shrieking sound filled the air, and it flooded down towards the forest.

Towards the Guardians.

"No," I whispered, then whirled to face all the terrified wolves behind me. "Run! All of you run to the Boglands, and don't look back!"

The Guardians took off fleeing as one into the forest. Only the Power-Holders and Power-Holders in training remained.

"We will fight," Boulder said determinedly.

Then, out of nowhere, a jet of lightning struck the forest. A fire began to blaze.

"Fight for our home!" Oriole howled.

I noticed a falling, flaming tree limb directly above him. "Oriole!" I screeched, lunging at my mentor. I knocked him back, then had to fling myself out of the way of the branch.

Smoke filled the air, and I gasped, hacking, trying to breath. *Where are the others?!*

I saw the shapes of three wolves up ahead. They turned and padded off.

"Wait!" I bounded after them. "Come back!" I dodged flames and more falling branches, the wolves just up ahead…

With a gasp, my paws hit something hard. I stumbled to the dirt, momentarily stunned.

Crawling over to the stone that had tripped me, I saw that the paw prints of three wolves were engraved in it.

"Delta." I looked up to see the older wolf, Shade. "You have done so much, but this will be your true test."

"But you can do it," Copper, the russet male wolf, said, "You are not alone."

"Never give up." The black she-wolf, Willow, faced me. Then all three wolves' eyes began to glow.

"Stand on the stone, Delta," Willow said.

I obeyed, then gasped as power flowed from each wolf… to me. A tingling sensation crawled across my fur, and golden light blinded my eyes.

Then it stopped.

I staggered off the stone, wondering what had just happened. "What did you do?" Then I realized that Shade, Copper, and Willow were gone.

"Delta!" Oriole bounded into the clearing. "The darkness is destroying the forest! I can't find the others!" Then he gasped, staring at me. "I sense something. You have power."

"The three wolves came to me," I said, dazed, "they did something. I feel… different."

"They clearly decided you were ready," my mentor said, a proud look in his eyes, "you know the spells, Delta. Use them."

I exhaled slowly, then looked up. Through the smoke, I could see the darkness. I could tell it was eating up the forest. I had to hurry!

"Fur to feathers, scales to skin! Change me on the outside, but not from within!" I shouted, imagining what I could be.

What I *would* be.

My body changed. I spread two massive wings out, and shuffled my sharp talons, snapping my beak. Then I shot into the sky.

I'll just stay a hawk forever. I thought as I soared above the forest. I could see the darkness.

I knew what had to be done, then.

Folding my wings, I dove, heading for the black cloud of death.

Delta, what are you doing?!

I paused, seeing Oriole and the Power-Holders, as hawks, soaring towards me. *What needs to be done. My light will defeat the darkness.*

Then Oriole beat his wings at me, almost making me fall out of the sky. *This is not your destiny, Delta. It is ours.*

No. I stared at my mentor in horror. *No. No!*

Most of the Power-Holders dove toward the darkness, vanishing inside. I could hear them screaming, but the darkness faltered.

"NO!" I shrieked, struggling to get to them, but Oriole, Sunshine, and Stone held me back.

It was an honor to train you, Delta. Sunshine tore toward the darkness, Stone right behind her.

Please, Oriole! I tried to reach him, but he used his power to create an invisible barrier.

I couldn't have asked for a better student, Delta. He blinked at me. *And the Guardians couldn't have a better leader to guide them out of this dark time.*

Then he dove.

Watching as he fell. Hearing the screams. Blasted backward through the air.

I fell toward the earth, morphing back into a wolf. With a muffled screech, I hit the ground.

22

With a gasp, I leaped to my paws. The fire was gone. In fact, the *forest* was gone.

And there were nine bodies nearby.

"No, no, no!" I pounded over to the wolves that I had learned with, trained with. I collapsed at Lemon's side. "Lemon!"

The blonde she-wolf blinked her eyes open. "Still here."

Sunflower, Reed and Boulder all groaned, picking themselves off the ground.

But the others didn't.

Ruby. Goldenrod. Dewdrop. Elderberry.

They were dead.

"Delta…" Sky's voice was weak. Her black fur was burned nearly off. I immediately knew that she wouldn't make it, but I still had to try!

"Broken skin, come together, may your wounds be healed and whole." Nothing happened. I shook my head desperately. "No! Broken skin, come together—"

"It's okay, Delta," Sky choked out. Her blind eyes seemed to know exactly where I was. "I forgive you, if you forgive me."

"Of course!" I whimpered. "It was an honor to fight beside you."

She didn't answer. She couldn't. It was over.

Oriole. The other nine Power-Holders. Most of my fellow pups. Sky.

They were all gone. And Peak…

I clenched my teeth. He'd done this. He'd infected our home with his blackness. Did he even know what he had done?

Nearby, Lemon staggered to her paws, joining Sunflower, Boulder, and Reed. "We should bury the dead."

"Of course," I mumbled. "But we should wait until the Guardians return, so they can say a final goodbye. These pups had parents."

"Oriole and the others?" Sunflower asked. When I shook my head, she crouched low to the ground, face full of sorrow.

"You're our leader now, Delta," Reed dipped his head to me.

"I'm still a pup!" I objected, but Lemon stopped me.

"You're our leader now that Oriole's… gone." She choked on a sob, then continued. "We will need new Power-Holders now that…" She couldn't finish, but turned and padded away.

I hung my head. What had become of the peaceful life I had once known? It had been ripped apart. At least Poppy was safe, I hoped.

Then I thought of Cynthia and my parents. They would be proud, but worried for me.

"It's time for another change, I guess," Boulder said quietly.

He was right. I stared up at the sky as a light snow began to fall on this now-barren plain. "The Guardians will rise above this."

The Guardians returned, horrified at what had happened. We buried the bodies of the six brave— but still way too young— wolves that had died. There was nothing left of Oriole and the nine Power-Holders to bury.

Birch and Mistflower each nuzzled my shoulder as we prepared to return to High Mountain. Cynthia met my eyes, and I knew she felt the same pain that I, and every other wolf, felt.

We padded up the secret tunnel, me in the lead. No wolves had objected to a pup becoming leader. They somehow had faith in me.

That meant I could have faith in myself.

Our home looked just like it had before. The Guardian Stone's blue light reached to all corners of the Crystal Cavern. It wasn't until I went down the tunnel that led to the Mystic Cave, alone, that I saw a solid slab of stone had sealed the entrance. The Crystal Dais was lost.

With a heavy sigh, I returned the way I had come. Now I wouldn't be able to get advice from Oriole. I still had to be strong, though, because some wolf had to lead the Guardians out of this disaster, and that wolf was me.

Years later…

I sat at the base of the Guardian Stone, watching as the Guardians milled about. High Mountain had been peaceful with me as leader, and the other nine Power-Holders.

Two of those wolves were actually padding up at that moment…

"Delta!" Lemon said cheerfully, padding across an arch.

"Lemon," I greeted the blonde-furred she-wolf, then turned to the white wolf at her side, "and Boulder. How has the hunting been?"

"Excellent!" Lemon replied, just as bouncy and bubbly as usual. "This spring will be a plentiful one."

As they padded off, I slowly wagged my tail. They really were quite a pair. Sometimes I thought about finding myself a wolf…

But then I remembered Peak.

Regret twisted around and around in my brain. At least now he couldn't hurt anyone else. If only I'd been able to save him…

Shaking all unhappy thoughts from my head, I closed my eyes, ready to take a little nap. It *had* been a long day.

I was standing in a dark, small burrow. A gray-furred she-wolf sat nearby, grooming a tiny gray she-pup.

"What should I name you?" She asked the pup, tickling her with her tail.

Then I saw the pup as a full-grown wolf. Her confident stance. Her piercing blue eyes.

She reminded me of a past Guardian that I had never truly gotten to meet.

"Willow," I whispered, gazing down at the tiny bundle of fur. "You look like a Willow."

Then Delta awoke, and somewhere, in a large forest far away, the gray she-wolf made the choice to call her new pup Willow.

EPILOGUE

I sat up and blinked. Where was I? Trees surrounded me on all sides, glittering as a slight breeze shook them. The ground was warm beneath my paws, yet frost seemed to cover it.

I was in the Crystal Forest.

A pond lay before me. I peered inside, gasping as I saw my dead body slumped next to Peak's. A gray she-wolf crouched by my side, along with Cynthia.

I was dead. I had joined the Unending Cycle.

I never had been very good at fighting.

"Delta." A she-wolf with long gray fur just like mine padded into the clearing.

"Mother!" I turned to touch Mistflower's cheek with my muzzle. "I have to go back! Willow needs me!"

She gazed at me sadly. Another wolf padded up—Birch. "It is too late, Delta," my father said softly, "you are dead. Your body, that is."

"Don't worry about Willow," a red-furred wolf with green eyes stood beside me, "she is strong."

"Oriole!" My heart swelled with joy at the sight of my long-dead mentor. "You're right, of course. Willow can lead the Guardians."

"With Shadow at her side, nothing is impossible," a russet male wolf strode into view, "as long as they stick together, the world has hope."

"You must be Bramble," I greeted my sister's mate, then looked around for Poppy… Pumpkin.

But she was nowhere to be seen.

Then I saw more wolves sitting around me. Sky was there, her black pelt clean and smooth. To my relief, she nodded at me, no anger in her now-clear eyes.

"Delta!"

I could hear Willow calling me, but couldn't answer. I peered at her shape in the pond as it began to blur. "Stay strong," I whispered, "the Ending is near."

Then I turned away from the water with a flick of my tail.

All the wolves were gone now— except for one. His gray fur was no longer clumped with blood. His murky green eyes were haunted, and yet there was something else in them. Something I hadn't seen in a long time.

Hope.

"Peak." I crept to his side. "She *will* defeat Scar."

He closed his eyes. "I know."

I was tempted to stay in this clearing with him, but I knew that I had other things to think about. Though it was my time to rest, that didn't mean that I wouldn't guide Willow's paw steps while I was at it…

THE END

THE WORLD IS IN DANGER, AND ONLY ONE YOUNG WOLF CAN CHANGE THINGS

THE GUARDIAN TRILOGY

Book One: THE CALLING

Willow is a young wolf living in Night Forest. Her life is pretty normal, but then something happens that turns her world upside down. She has a vision in which a she-wolf calls her to High Mountain. Willow sets out, unaware that she is being thrust into a crucial role in a war against good and evil.

Book Two: THE UNKNOWN

Willow and Shadow find themselves hopelessly lost in the Unknown Lands. They know that if they don't reach High Mountain soon, terrible prices will be paid: The blood of wolves.

Book Three: THE ENDING

The Guardians face off against the Dark Wolves for the final time. Only one side will live. Blood will be spilt. Willow knows that to save the world, she has to fight harder than she's ever fought before. Who will rise? Who will end it all?

READ THEM ALL!

www.ingramcontent.com/pod-product-compliance
Lightning Source LLC
LaVergne TN
LVHW010557160826
845677LV00013B/3164

* 9 7 9 8 3 6 8 1 6 0 8 0 1 *